Welcome to New Sherlock Holmes Mysteries -

"The best-selling series of new Sherlock Holmes stories. All faithful to The Canon."

Each story is a tribute to one of the sixty original stories about the world's most famous detective. If you are encountering these new stories for the first time, start with *Studying Scarlet,* and keep going.
(https://www.amazon.com/dp/B07CW3C9YZ)

If you subscribe to Kindle Unlimited, then you can 'borrow for free' every one of the books.

They are all available as ebooks, paperbacks, hardcovers, and in large print.

Check them out at
www.SherlockHolmesMysteries.com.

The Bald-
Headed Trust

A New Sherlock Holmes Mystery #4

Craig Stephen Copland

Published by:
Conservative Growth
1101 30th Street NW
Washington, DC 20007

Cover design by Rita Toews

ISBN-10:   1500394211

ISBN-13:   978-1500394219

Dedication

With apologies to Sir Arthur Conan Doyle, and with profound respect and admiration for the saints within the religious movement known as the Plymouth Brethren

Contents

Acknowledgments

I discovered *The Adventures of Sherlock Holmes* while a student at Scarlett Heights Collegiate Institute in Toronto. My English teachers – Bill Stratton, Norm Oliver, and Margaret Tough – inspired me to read and write. I shall be forever grateful to them.

The plot of this novella is adapted freely from Conan Doyle's *The Red-Headed League*. The idea for the diabolical crime was borrowed from the fascinating book, *Flash Boys* by Michael Lewis. I merely transferred the crime back one hundred and twenty-five years to the time of Sherlock Holmes.

My dearest and best friend, Mary Engelking, read all drafts, helped with whatever historical and geographical accuracy was required, and offered insightful recommendations for changes to the narrative structure, characters, and dialogue. Thank you.

I am indebted also to Rev. Dr. Max S. Weremchuk of Kerzenheim, Germany (formerly of Niagara-on-the-Lake, Ontario, Canada) for the scholarly information he generously provided concerning the Plymouth Brethren sect and John Nelson Darby.

For the very idea of writing a new Sherlock Holmes mystery I thank the Bootmakers, the Sherlockian Society of Toronto.

Chapter One

To Plymouth

The spring and summer of 1890 were quite tumultuous in London and on the continent. Some of these events led me to marvel at the scientific progress that was sweeping all of Western Civilization. Others left me with a deep sense of foreboding. The young emperor of Germany, Kaiser Bill as we called him, summarily fired the old chap, Bismarck, who had guided Germany through its unification. Great Britain, France, and Germany continued their scramble for Africa, claiming and swapping vast expanses of desert, shorelines, islands, and jungles.

The Scottish engineers opened the Firth of Forth Bridge in Edinburgh, the largest in the British Empire at that time. All over the world governments and companies were laying undersea telegraph cables. Several had been strung between North America and England, and Canada just announced a new link to Bermuda. The masses of London continued to flock to hear lectures by Henry Morton Stanley in Albert Hall. He had led a disastrous expedition into Egypt and had been roundly condemned by the Royal Society, but that did not stop

Londoners, from the lowliest ostler all the way to the Queen herself, from marveling at his tales of Pygmies and cannibals and treks through Darkest Africa.

I had that spring, to some considerable acclaim, published in *Lippincott's* the second of my stories about the adventures of my friend and exceptional detective, Sherlock Holmes, and by the Fall, his name and reputation had become widely known throughout the country. I, or any reasonable man, might have thought that such recognition would have made him happy. It did not. He was quite the opposite. Since his rescuing of Violet Hunter and Alice Rucastle in March, he had not had a single case that demanded the application of his special province of logical deduction. I feared that he might again lapse into the use of his dangerous seven percent solution, and taxed my brain for some diversion that might occupy his imagination.

I settled on the idea of a short holiday to the seashore. I had not been to sea since returning from Afghanistan, and Holmes had little or no use for the beauty of the ocean or any other part of Nature for that matter. But I pointed out to him that a very high proportion of criminals and of his clients had spent some time at sea, and that it would be an excellent opportunity for him to learn more about seafarers and their ways if we were to spend a fortnight relaxing in the port city of Plymouth. The majestic Duke of Cornwall Hotel was advertising late-season rates and featuring excellent fresh seafood from the Grand Banks. After some exasperating negotiations Holmes finally agreed to a single week, and so began what turned into the *Mystery of the Bald-Headed Trust.*

On Monday, October 14 we rose early, took a cab to Paddington and boarded *The Flying Dutchman.* For several decades, it had made the journey along what some wags had called *God's Wonderful Railway* but which the rest of us knew as the Great Western. In just under five hours the powerful new *Royal Cornwall,* a sleek Dean Single 3031 Class locomotive thundered its way southwest to Plymouth. I made some attempt to draw Holmes into friendly conversation, but he was having none of it. He sat in silence, staring out the windows. He only spoke to me once and it was to say, in a grave voice, "My dear Watson, I know you are trying your best to be a good sport and make this a pleasant outing, and I can only ask that you forgive my melancholy mood. However my mind is consumed with the stories I have heard most recently about a syndicate of very evil men who are spreading their web through England, Europe, and America. They will stop at nothing: not murder, blackmail, nor treason to reap their ill-gotten gains. I fear it will be only a matter of time before I am called upon to lock horns with the mastermind of their nest of vipers. These few days respite may be the last I am able to indulge in for months, or perhaps years to come."

"Oh come, come, Holmes," I said with feigned cheerfulness, "we are going to be in sleepy old Plymouth. Nothing dastardly there ever happens except for an occasional sailor stealing a barrel of rum. Banish all evil doers from your mind and refresh your spirits. At least that way you will be physically and mentally restored to better fight your foes upon your return to London."

He smiled warmly at me. "Thank you, my good friend. You are very kind to look out for my well-being. You do a rather better job of it than I do myself. I will do my best to be a cheerful companion for the duration of our little holiday."

As I expected, he immediately returned to his quiet scowl and said nothing more until noon, when we arrived at the shabby shed of Millbay Station in Plymouth.

Having secured our suite of rooms at the Duke of Cornwall, I insisted on our taking a good brisk walk along the seashore and harbor. I guided him along the grand parade, past the historic Smeaton Lighthouse, around the curve of the Admiralty and gave a nod to the splendid Royal William Yard. Having read some of the Cooks guidebook concerning Plymouth, I chatted about each site and its place in history. "Just think Holmes," I remarked, "it was two hundred and seventy years ago that the *Mayflower* departed from this very harbor."

3

Holmes said nothing. The discovery and settling of America did not strike him as a historical event worth celebrating.

He stopped however at the Telegraph Wharf and looked upon the parade of shops that had recently been erected there. A smile of bemusement flicked at the corners of his mouth. I looked at the shops and noticed *The Jolly Jack Public House,* an office of the American firm, *Western Union,* a small store calling itself *The Little Flock Christian Book and Bible Shop,* the harbor branch of Baring's Bank, a vegetarian restaurant, and a carriage repair shop. I could see nothing at all that struck me as the least bit amusing.

"Pray tell, Holmes. What do you find to smile at when you look at what, as far as I can tell, is a very ordinary collection of new shops and services?"

"It is only my idle amusing of myself, Watson, but I am looking upon *damnation, communication, salvation, pecuniation, vegetation, and transportation* all in one row. Silly of me isn't it? But it is curious that all these enterprises manage to exist packed in together. What I found most striking was the proximity of the store selling Bibles to the pub. I rather fear that the effect of the one would be canceled out by the other."

"Oh, Holmes," I smiled back at him. "I had not thought of it that way, but I am sure you are quite right."

"Yes, Watson. This sleepy city of Plymouth has, if I remember correctly, quite a history as a haven of rowdy drunken sailors, side by side with the most intense religious revivals. That strikes me as an excellent formula for the fomenting of unusual criminal activities but, most regrettably, I have not been following the Plymouth press recently and so have heard of nothing. Very well, let us go and find our dinner and perhaps the library at the hotel will have some acceptable reading material."

With this, we left the harbor area and returned to the hotel for a pleasant howbeit entirely uneventful evening.

4

That night I slept that sleep that knits up the raveled sleeve of care and did not rise until well after eight o'clock. Holmes was already up and out of the hotel by the time I emerged from my room and so I contented myself with a late breakfast and settled in the sunny parlor to catch up on the past three volumes of *The Lancet.*

It was late morning before Sherlock Holmes returned, and what a change had come over him. He not only had some color in his cheeks from the morning sun and crisp seaside air, but there was once again that bounce in his step and his eyes were shining brightly between puckered lids. I recognized that look and knew straight away that it had nothing to do with the scenic vistas of the Atlantic Ocean.

"Good morning, Holmes," I said, a little slyly. "I see that your seaside holiday in the beauty of Nature is working wonders on your health and disposition."

"Oh, my good Doctor. You know perfectly well that I do not care a fig for the beauties of Nature. But you are totally correct in seeing that I am enjoying my holiday. However, I assure you that it is only because my holiday has ceased to be a holiday and has turned into a most interesting adventure."

"Jolly good for whatever reason. I am pleased for anything that has been such a tonic to you. But pray you, do tell what happened during the past four hours to dispel the melancholy."

"Very well," he said. "I slept rather poorly in a strange bed, alternately cursing the cacophony of squawking seagulls and the booming sound of the ships' horns as they made their way in and out of the harbor. So, at first light, I went for a walk through the town, if for no other reason than to acquire some additional knowledge of this uninspiring city. I found myself back at the Telegraph Wharf that I had thought to be amusing during our stroll last evening. I hoped, in vain it turned out, that the pub might be serving tea and breakfast, but on entering found only the cleaning staff and rather unpleasant odors of

5

stale beer, urine and vomit from the night before — the smell that inhabits all pubs in the first hours of the morning after.

"The door to the shop selling religious books, however, was open, and having nothing better to do I entered and thought that, at the least, I could add to my knowledge of emerging spiritualist movements that have affected, or perhaps I should say afflicted, so many gullible folks of late. I entered and saw that the place was clean and orderly, and well-stocked with books, religious tracts, hymn books and various religious paraphernalia such as wall plaques bearing scripture verses, Bible knowledge quiz games, and paintings of the Lord as if he were the pilot of a ship, with a hand on the shoulder of a young man behind the ship's wheel.

"The proprietor was a youngish woman, I estimate in her late twenties. I can only describe her as plain but handsome. Tall and sturdy. She had the red hair of a Highland lass, but it was all bundled up into braids and wound about the top of her head. If ever it were to be let down and taken out of braids I imagine it would extend well down past the small of her back. Her skin was pale, as is common to redheads, but her complexion flawless, rendering her blue eyes quite striking. Her countenance was rather perfectly balanced, but she made no effort at all to enhance it. She had not a speck of powder or paint upon her, no jewelry, and no colorful or stylish clothing such as you would normally see on an attractive young woman. Her plain white dress covered her from her neck to her wrists and indicated an obsessive modesty.

"Assuming her to be no more than a sad Reformist Protestant who was their equivalent of a nun, I ignored her and perused the bookshelves. The shop had some excellent works by St. Augustine, an entire set of Calvin's Institutes, the collected sermons of Dr. Spurgeon and a rather wide assortment of books by John Nelson Darby, Anthony Norris Groves, and George Mueller. Are you familiar with them?

"A very little," I replied. "Are they not some of the leading lights of one of the puritanical sects of evangelicals?"

"Yes. Precisely. And their movement has had particular popularity here in Plymouth. I confess that my indulgence in some of the pleasant vices that they condemn would exclude me forever from their ranks, as became abundantly obvious when I sat in one of their chairs to look through a volume of biography and prepared to enjoy at least one pipe of fine tobacco."

"Oh oh," I interjected. "I gather the good Christian shop lady was not pleased with that prospect."

"Not at all," Holmes replied. "But her words both surprised and annoyed me. She said, 'You do know, Mr. Sherlock Holmes, that your body is the temple of the Holy Spirit and you would be a healthier man and a better detective if you ceased breathing poisons into it.' Now, at first, I was a little annoyed, and not pleased with being deprived of the joy of tobacco. I also had some unkind thoughts about you, my dear friend, for publishing that story and giving me such notoriety that even shop ladies in Plymouth would recognize me. She continued giving me her little talking to and said, 'You are quite welcome to stay and read, but we will not allow our premises to be fouled by tobacco smoke.' Before I could think up some snide rejoinder, she then gave me a warm smile and proceeded to say, 'Please forgive my forwardness, sir, but my curiosity will not permit me to refrain from asking you how it is that London's famous detective is to be found in a Christian bookstore in Plymouth so early on a fall morning?'"

"So I gave her a less than entirely courteous but utterly truthful reply about being here on holiday, replaced the volume I had been looking into, and made a move towards the door.

"Well, didn't she give me quite the sideways look as if she did not believe a word I said, and then she posed a very interesting question about one of the details in your story."

"And which was that?" I asked.

"Oh, it matters not, for it was only the first question she asked. Then, without a trace of guile, she began to ask more. All along the line of 'Why did I not do this?' or 'Why had I failed to do that?' And when she was finished with the events recorded in *The Sign of the Four* she began in on other cases that had been reported in *The Times* in which I had some degree of involvement. And then she began on yet more cases on which I had not been consulted. Her interrogation of me was entirely without pretense, but I have never been so thoroughly taken to task. The woman had not only read every page of the reports in *The Times,* but she quite clearly had remembered every detail. And when she had exhausted the Crime Section she moved on and began asking me what I thought about the Germans and their new Chancellor, and the foreign policies of Lord Salisbury, and the Italians in Abyssinia, and the French in the Sudan, and the renunciation of polygamy by the Mormons in America. And if that were not enough she quizzed me further about the recent policy changes in the Bank of England, and trade with the Cape Colony, and if I believed that investing in shares of the company formed by W. B. Purvis to manufacture his newly patented fountain pen would be a wise choice or, given the topsy-turvy state of world affairs, should people just stick to gold.

"You can imagine that I was quite intrigued by this woman and eventually remarked to her that I had not expected a member of a devout sect to be so informed and concerned with the things of the world. She gave me a puzzled look and told me in quite a matter-of-fact way that to be an effective witness for the Lord one simply had to live with the Bible tucked under one arm and *The Times* under the other. I said that I was quite sure she was correct and I admit to you, Watson, that I refrained from saying that I might find occasional substitutes for Holy Writ. But then it was my turn to quiz this remarkable young woman.

"I asked her numerous questions about Plymouth, and about the harbor, and the shipments that moved in and out of here. Again she amazed me with her answers. She knew the names, schedules, and ports of call of every major trading vessel; of the shipments they were importing and exporting, and for which British firms they were intended. In passing, she noted that any astute investor should be looking into shares of the Armstrong Whitworth Co., who were sending armaments all over the Empire. She had bought a few shares of the company for her husband and herself, noting that while her faith would not permit her to invest in highly profitable manufacturers of whiskey and tobacco products, the provision of arms to those who were protecting the Empire was a calling ordained by the Lord Himself.

"So there you have it, Watson. If we invest our savings in armaments we shall be able to enjoy our retirement, for the dividends shall never cease as long as the Empire prevails and the rest of the world detests it.

"After over an hour of this delightful conversation I rose to leave and she gave me quite a hard look and said, 'This has been a wonderful opportunity for me, sir, as my chances to have the insights of such a well-informed gentleman are rare. However, I have to ask you, bold though it may seem, what your opinion is of the Telegraph Murders that took place here recently, as I assume that they are the true reason for your being on Telegraph Wharf and that your so-called holiday is merely a somewhat flimsy excuse.'"

"Ah yes, Holmes," I interjected. "I read of that event in the papers, but neither of us took any notice of it as it happened in the West and not in London."

"Exactly, Watson. I had to confess to the woman, that truthfully my visit to Plymouth had nothing to do with any crime at all, and that it was, quite frankly, only for a few days respite. And that furthermore, other than what I had read in the brief report in the Press I knew very little, but that I would be most eager if I could learn more, and would she be so kind as to enlighten me.

"She raised her eyebrows ever so slightly, but I gather that she discerned that I was being truthful and told me that she was quite concerned about it as she had been personally acquainted with the victims and that the crime had occurred only a few blocks away from her shop.

"The two men who had been murdered were family men from Glasgow. They were communications engineers who were under contract to the Western Union Company to assist in the installation of the new office that is adjacent to their bookstore. Both men were in their thirties and appeared to be dour, clean-living men who worked late into the evening, and then made their way directly back to their rooming house without stopping in at the *Jolly Jack* or any other public house for a pint before taking their dinner at their lodgings.

"On one or two occasions each of them had wandered into her shop but she felt it was out of boredom rather than any spiritual yearning. They had chatted briefly with her and her husband and left without buying anything. Then three weeks ago both were found lying dead in a lane off of Battery Street, not far from their rooming house. No one had heard any gunshots. No bands of thugs had been seen in the area. No one knew of anything these men could have been involved in that was in the least untoward. Their wallets had been emptied, but their watches left behind, leaving the police to assume that robbery was only a ruse to distract the investigation. To this day, the police continue to describe the event as 'By Persons Unknown' and 'For Causes Unknown.'

"It was terribly upsetting, she said, to the other merchants in the parade of stores along the Wharf. They had all recently set up shop, were all on good terms with each other, and had not had enough time to start to quarrel. The Western Union Company, being a very wealthy American firm and with a sincere sense of compassion, had looked after all funeral arrangements and set up a generous pension for the men's families even though, by law, they were not required to since the men had only been under contract and not employees. To this day, nothing more is known. My appearance in the lady's shop this morning was, she had assumed, connected to the murders and she concluded that I had been called upon to consult with the local constabulary.

"I acknowledged, somewhat apologetically, that I had not been and that the police did not know that I was here in Plymouth. I assured her, however, that I would avail myself of the opportunity and hoped that presently I would be asked to assist. I bid this fascinating woman good morning and promptly walked over to the police station. The local chaps there graciously welcomed me, repeated the details that the woman had already given me, and invited my participation.

"As a result, Watson, this holiday is not a useless waste of time at all. It has become an adventure that may keep us here for some time to come, and as long as you do not impose upon me any more hours of staring out to sea, my holiday may yet become memorable and enjoyable."

Chapter Two

The Telegraph Murders

olmes said nothing more. When lunch was served, he ate quickly and I could see that the lust of the chase had overtaken him. His brilliant reasoning powers were being summoned and I knew that an evil time would soon be coming upon those whom he had set himself to hunt down.

He spent the next two hours poring over the reports that the police had given to him. He perused maps of the city and copies of the local newspaper from the days after the incident, which the front desk of *The Duke* has efficiently procured for him. On three occasions he set down the materials, lit a pipe, closed his eyes, pressed his fingertips together, and entered his familiar pose of burning concentration. I knew that he would snap back at me in anger if I were to disturb him and so left him alone, but in my heart, I was quite thrilled to see him back in his favorite role of the relentless sleuth-hound, the keen-witted, ready-handed consulting detective.

I was not paying sufficient attention, otherwise I would have cut off the young bell boy who had the misfortune to interrupt him. "Mr. Holmes," the lad announced, "a letter for you," and he placed a silver tray bearing an envelope in front of the detective, and had the further gall to place his young hand on Holmes's shoulder and give him a bit of a shake as one would give to a guest who had decided that the parlor of the hotel was an acceptable spot to take one's afternoon nap.

"Confound you!" Holmes exploded. "Cannot you see that I am working? Do not ever, ever disturb me like this again. Now get you gone and do not let me see your face again!"

The poor lad was visibly upset by Holmes's reaction. His face became distraught and I feared he would break into tears. I immediately interposed myself and took him by the arm and led him away a few steps to safety. "Please young man," I consoled him. "Do not worry about the reaction of my colleague. He has a very intense character. I will look after the letter. Now you get along and do not worry about it for another minute." I gave the boy two shillings, for which he thanked me and left, but not before giving a frightened glance back at Sherlock Holmes, who had once again retreated into his near trance. I rather suspected that no more letters would be hand-delivered by anyone on the attentive staff.

I sat down and took the liberty of opening the letter on Holmes's behalf. Upon finishing it, I sat up straight in my chair, took a deep breath and in a voice that is usually only heard from sergeant majors, announced, "Holmes! Wake up! This is urgent and you have to pay attention and listen at once."

His reaction was instant and predictable. However, I had been the recipient of his temper on more than one occasion in the past and knew that his bark would be far worse than his bite, particularly after he was forced to listen to the contents of the letter.

"Blast you, Watson!" he snapped. "You, of all people, should know that I am not to be disturbed!"

"And you, of all people, Sherlock Holmes," I snapped back, "should know that I would not do so if whatever I hold in my hand were not of critical importance to your case!"

That shut him up, or at least diminished his reaction to a glare.

"This letter is from the *Little Flock Christian Bookstore* and it bears on the Telegraph Murders. Do you wish me to read it to you, or shall I just send it up to our rooms and have it placed in your luggage?"

His glare softened. "Very well, Watson. I apologize for my rudeness and unkind words. Please, my friend, be so kind as to read the letter to me. I assume it is from the lady that I spoke with this morning."

"You assume wrongly," I said, with perhaps an unkind trace of smugness. "It is from her husband and both of them may be in some danger." Now that got his attention and he gave it entirely to me and the piece of paper in my hand.

The letter ran as follows:

Dear Mr. Sherlock Holmes:

This morning you visited our shop and conversed with my wife, Mrs. Miriam Darby. She wisely did not disclose all aspects of the connection of our family to the Telegraph Murders before committing it to a short season of prayer and of discussing it with me.

My wife is a most remarkable woman and in addition to having an exceptional knowledge of history, commerce, and commercial affairs, she has been given by the Holy Ghost the spiritual gift of the discerning of spirits . . .

Here I stopped. "I must say, Holmes, are you sure that this woman is not some sort of fanciful spiritualist? I am not familiar with any medical condition known as a gift for the discerning of spirits."

"In truth, my good Doctor, you are highly familiar with it and you have a rather good case of it yourself."

"I beg your pardon, Holmes. I have no such thing."

"Oh come now. If a man approaches you and tells you that he has a horse for sale, how do you decide whether to send him away or listen to him?"

"I do not know. I guess it would be based on whether or not I trusted the man; if he gave me a sense of being truthful, or of being a scoundrel."

"And on what would you draw to form such an immediate conclusion?" Holmes pressed me.

"I suppose on my years of working with a great many men in the army, as a medical doctor, and even from observing so many of your clients."

"Precisely. And if the horse were offered for sale to Mrs. Hudson, would she be taken in by a swindler?"

"Of course not. Her woman's intuition is highly refined and she would see through such a man in a moment."

You are absolutely correct, Watson," Holmes continued. "And what if it were me? I have neither your vast experience of dealing with men, nor one ounce of woman's intuition. But still I would form a conclusion. How could that be?"

I shrugged my shoulders. "You would use you powers and processes of observation and scientific reason."

"Exactly, my good man. All these ways of reaching conclusions, that we call by different names, are the same thing. Some people have a well-developed sense of the motives of other people and some will be forever dupes. This very Christian lady gave me quite the going over this morning and I do not believe I could have deceived her even with my best disguise. She modestly attributes her gifts to supernatural forces. It matters not their origin, they are nonetheless present. Pray, continue reading."

I continued:

. . . of the discerning of spirits
and she knew in her heart that you
had been sent to us by God as an
answer to our prayers.

I stopped again, unable to resist. "My word, Holmes, did you sprout wings and a halo? I never knew. Why did you not tell me of your promotion?"

"Enough Watson. Get on with it."

. . . Her spirit has told her that our
family may be in danger and that the men
who committed the murders are known to us
and may do us harm. I beseech you to
forgive our intruding on your holiday,
but I am requesting a brief audience with
you so that we may ask for your advice.

Yours sincerely,

Jabez Nelson Darby,
Owner,
Little Flock Christian Bookstore,
Telegraph Wharf, Plymouth.

"There is something quite strangely appealing about this whole affair, would you not agree, Watson? Please be so kind as to send a note off to Mr. Darby, asking him to come and see us here as soon as possible."

I took a moment at the writing desk in the bay window of the hotel, wrote the requested note, and went to find the bell boy, who, for good reason, had not returned to the part of the room in which we were sitting.

Within thirty minutes a young gentleman appeared in the entrance to the parlor. The bellboy pointed him in our direction. He was a pleasant-looking man of perhaps thirty years of age, with a thin frame and face and a bit of a stoop to his posture. He was dressed in a modest, but clean and well-pressed suit, such as one might expect of an earnest owner of a bookstore. Oddly, he had not removed his hat upon entering the premises of the grand hotel and approached Holmes and I with it still upon his head.

"Mr. Holmes, and Dr. Watson?" he asked politely.

"You have found us," I assured him. "May I ask the boy to bring us a cup of tea? You are looking a little concerned and I gather you have come here in haste."

"Why bless you, Doctor. That would be wonderful. Indeed, I did hurry and I beg you to forgive my intruding on your holidays. I gather it is a rather rare event in your busy lives."

"Fortunately, you are correct. They are rare," said Holmes. "And your intrusion and the reasons for it are the best thing to have happened in an otherwise tedious expedition. Please be seated and tell me, as frankly as you can, what it is that is besetting your good self and your remarkable wife."

He pulled up a chair, sat down, removed his hat and placed it in his lap. The eyes of both Holmes and I went immediately to the top of his head. There was not a single hair upon it. He was as completely bald as a newborn babe. He could see us staring and I felt embarrassed by our rude behavior. Holmes, who was never one to be overly tactful, ignored all manners and simply asked him, "What in the world happened to your hair?"

The young man blushed momentarily and I detected a flash of pain in his face. But he quickly recovered and smiled a little mischievously back at Sherlock Holmes and said, "You are the great detective. You tell me. I can't seem to find it anywhere. Perhaps you could track it down and return it to me."

Both Holmes and I laughed at his good natured and witty reply. "I deduce," said Holmes, continuing with the pleasant tone, "that you experienced a serious medical condition recently and that your fine head of hair vacated itself. You appear to have recovered from whatever it was that beset you, but your hair has not yet been so informed and still is in hiding."

The man laughed and smiled back. "You are entirely correct. For a period of over a year, I suffered from a terrible bout of brain fever. I lost weight, all my energy, any ability to laugh, and all my hair. My spirits have finally been restored."

Here he paused, and then continued, "But once again I find myself deeply troubled and fearful, as is my wife, and that is what brings me to speak with you. Again, I apologize for disturbing you but we have nowhere else to turn and your arrival in our shop this morning was indeed a godsend."

"I have been called few things any better," said Holmes, "and many things much worse. If I am to be of any use to you and your wife please tell me your story and whatever possible connection you might have with these terrible and inexplicable murders. Please. You have our complete attention."

"As you know from my note, my name is Jabez Nelson Darby. You may have heard of my great-uncle, John Nelson Darby."

"Indeed," I said. "He was a rather distinguished Bible scholar and preacher. Did he not do a translation of the Bible from the original Hebrew and Greek entirely by himself? Is he still alive?"

"Yes. That is who he was, and sadly no, he passed on to glory several years ago, after a long a very fruitful life and ministry. He founded the movement that you may know as the Plymouth Brethren and one of the largest and most active assemblies of believers was started, under his oversight, here in Plymouth. Similar meetings have been formed throughout the world.

"He was a stern man in many ways, but he was a loving and devoted uncle to me and, in his later years, became convinced that his mantle would fall on me as Elijah's had on Elisha. He fully expected me to take up his leadership position in the movement and devote myself to Biblical scholarship, and teaching and preaching of the Word of God. I loved him dearly and did everything I could to live up to his expectations but, alas, I just do not have the mind or the disposition of a scholar, and I quake with terror when I am in front of a crowd of people and expected to give a word.

"The best I could do was to open a small bookstore here in Plymouth with the hope and prayer that it would be a witness and ministry to the many seamen who are constantly making their way through our streets as they come on and off of scores of merchant ships that dock in our harbor. When my uncle died, I was deeply saddened knowing that his wish to see me blessed in ministry was never fulfilled. It is hard to say why it had such an effect on my spirit, but I succumbed to a long bout of brain fever. For months after his death all my ambition, my cheerfulness, my desire for food and laughter all vanished. It was a daily struggle to get myself out of my bed in the morning, to try to show any attention and affection to my wonderful wife or our two small children. Many times I contemplated taking my own life and convinced myself that doing so would be the best favor I could bestow on my family so that they could be rid of me, and start over with someone who would not be such a burden to them.

"My wife, Miriam, who you met this morning, is an exceptional woman and I could not in my wildest dreams imagine having been blessed with so loving and caring and capable a helpmeet. She quite simply took over the business, looked after all the commercial affairs, managed the lives and schooling of the children and in short, carried me until my spirits slowly recovered. When she heard that there was to be new electrified building erected at Telegraph Wharf she immediately secured us one of the storefronts on the parade, knowing that it would not only give us a much more visible witness to the seamen, even those who were entering and leaving the *Jolly Jack,* but that a better location would cause our sales to rise and the book business, which is not lucrative at the best of times, to prosper. And indeed, it has. She was right. I have never in the seven years I have been married to her and the two years we courted, known her to be wrong.

"The events that my wife has discerned to have been connected to the murders began just over three months ago, on the first Sunday of July. As we do every Sunday, we came to meeting at the Gospel Hall for the service of the Lord's Supper and sat where we normally do every week, somewhat near to the back in case the children have to make an exit as children often have to do when required to sit still for over an hour.

"In front of us a few rows, I saw the strangest thing. There were two men, both dressed in dark suits, but whose heads were completely bald — exactly like mine. They did not stand and give a word or lead in prayer during the service, but they did partake of the elements, the bread and wine, as they were passed. When the service ended our leading elder stood to give the announcements and he acknowledged the presence of our visitors. They had brought with them a letter of commendation from an assembly in Brooklyn, New York, which the elder read aloud. These two men, Brother Ross Duncan and Brother Clayton Johns, were commended to our fellowship by the saints gathered in New York. After having been anointed with oil and prayed over, they had been miraculously cured of their severe medical condition. They experienced a call to missions and were given full-time commendation to ministry. They were on their way to help the work in the Faroe Islands but first would be spending a year in Plymouth where they would learn about the Brethren assembly movement and the truth of the dispensational understanding of the Word, as well as engage in a short task of Christian philanthropy to which they had also been called. And we were requested to receive them in the Lord and assist them in whatsoever business they had as becometh saints.

"As you might imagine their presence and their similarity to my condition was of intense interest to my wife, and she insisted that we wait at the back of the Hall after the service so that we could meet them. I had no desire to, as it was all I could manage to endure the service itself, and wanted to do nothing more than get back to my home and have a very long Sunday afternoon nap, but she prevailed.

"We met the two American men and had no more than introduced ourselves to each other and commented on the shared affliction of baldness, but one of the leading elders greeted us and insisted that we all come back to his home to enjoy Sunday dinner together. He was a very gracious and godly man and blessed by the Lord with material wealth, and it was his custom to invite visitors to the assembly back to his home. It was an invitation we could not refuse and so we went and enjoyed a pleasant dinner of roast beef and Yorkshire pudding that his lovely wife and the help had prepared. The children ate quickly and were given leave to play in the garden and we listened to the exceptional story of our visitors.

"They had both been dealt severe bouts of brain fever some three years ago and by chance, which they now acknowledged was divine providence, they met in the waiting room of the same doctor in the Gramercy area of Manhattan. They became friends, such as often happens among those who share similar afflictions, and would meet up from time to time for supper in the Greenwich Village part of the city. On one occasion, a Sunday evening, they were walking through the Bowery and heard the rousing joyful sounds of hymns being sung in one of the mission buildings. They entered, enjoyed the music and listened to the preaching of the Word of God. Having come under the sound of the Gospel, they were convicted in their hearts by the Holy Spirit and when the invitation was given to come forward and receive salvation, they both did so. Since getting saved they have been in fellowship in one of the Brethren assemblies in Brooklyn and have been blessed in all aspects of their lives, their health, and their income except, of course, for the restoration of their hair, which they claim as a badge of honor and note that it has become a surefire way to invite conversation, thus giving them an opportunity to share their testimonies.

"They had both felt the Macedonian call to mission work and were commended by the believers to do so, and were living by faith, depending on the Lord daily for their every need.

"Their reason for coming to Plymouth, they confided, was the result of a specific request from one of the men of the assembly. He had exceptional wealth and had, it turned out, suffered through a serious bout of brain fever himself many years ago. He felt a deep sympathy for men who were beset by this terrible sickness and had established a trust that aided medical research into the condition, along with the propagation of the gospel, so that men who were suffering so deeply might be cured in both their bodies and souls.

"My wife approved of this wise approach, combining as it did the most recent advances of medical science with the necessary ministry to the soul of man, and we had a friendly conversation. Twice that week they came to our home for tea and chatted further and they told us more about their work. They had been commissioned by the wealthy benefactor to register a similar charity here in England, to raise support for its work, and to get it started in its ministry to those men in need. They expected to have their work here finished within a year and then they would head on to the Faroe Islands.

"We wished them well and had a time of prayer together. Then the following week they came to me with looks of grave concern on their faces. It seems that the Office of the Public Trustee, the one that supervises British charities, does not permit those who are not British citizens to operate a charity. They particularly do not like it if Americans come across the pond, open a trust and assume that they can dictate its operations from Oshkosh, or some similar location. They had not expected to run into this roadblock. They had, they claimed, prayed about this issue and the Lord had given them the solution. They said that they would take over the temporary operations of my bookstore if I would serve as the founding general secretary of the charity. It would only be for a few months and I would have an office, which they had recently acquired, as well as a generous stipend of four pounds a week. They required no income for themselves since they were supported by the assemblies in Brooklyn.

"This appeared to us to be a gift from the Lord and we immediately accepted. In retrospect, it is a matter that we should have prayed over first. Had we done so, the events that followed might not have occurred.

"In mid-July, I presented myself to their new little office just off of Millbay Road. The sharp, bright sign on the door read *Gone Today, Hair Tomorrow – The Brain Fever Charitable Trust of England*. It was a witty and clever name and they put me to work writing out letters requesting gifts of funds from a long list of wealthy Christians throughout England. Each application was the same and I had to write it out over and over again with minor alternations depending on the relative wealth of the potential benefactor and any information they had secured on his previous gifts. They had quite a file and some excellent research on many wealthy people, and so I began to prepare the letters and submissions. They explained that I was engaging in what the American philanthropy industry called *grantsmanship*. I was unaware of the term or the practice but it was not difficult work and I felt that I was contributing to a good cause.

"The added benefit was that I was expected, as part of the letter and application, to include a personal word of testimony, sharing from my heart how I had suffered, and the ways in which both medicine and the blessings of the Lord were bringing about my healing. At first, it was quite a tribulation to me as I could not think of any good thing that had happened in my life recently. But as I persevered I acknowledged that my lovely wife had been a blessing from God, and so I wrote words to that effect in my testimony. But the next day I felt I could not just repeat what I had said the day before, and so I searched my soul for another small blessing in my life, and it became immediately clear to me that my beautiful children, my five-year-old son and three-year-old daughter, were an unmistakable sign of the Lord's blessing. And so it went.

"Each day I prayed and meditated and each day another blessing in my life was revealed to me, and so I wrote about it in the letters. I noted the blessings of my health, of my family, of my godly uncle, of my loving parents, of the sunrise over the ocean, of living in the British Empire, and of our gracious Queen. There were so many truly wonderful things that had enriched my life and for which I was moved to be profoundly grateful. The result of all this was that the dark cloud that had come with my brain fever slowly lifted. In addition to counting my blessings every day, I was heeding the advice of our good doctors and taking a brisk daily walk, eating plenteous fruit and vegetables, curtailing my intake of red meats, and getting regular sleep. My body was healthier than it had been in years. My spirit was alive with joy. I was moved to loving intimacy with my long-suffering wife and enjoyed times of play with my children such as I had never experienced.

"And the two Americans were doing wondrous things in the bookstore. Our sales had increased threefold. They appeared to have a gift of closing the sale, as they say. The shop appeared to be clean and well managed. Every Friday afternoon they would meet me and take from me the applications I had carefully and prayerfully prepared, saying that they had arranged a private delivery service so that they could be handed to the potential benefactors in total confidence and privacy, which they claimed was critical for the success of philanthropy.

"By the middle of September, the store had made a clear profit of one hundred pounds. I had been paid over thirty pounds by the Trust.

24

My astute wife invested the profits in some excellent public stock companies and we felt that we were enjoying the blessing of the Lord.

"Life could not have been better. But then, beginning about two weeks ago, some things started to change. It began one night as my dear wife and I were lying in bed prior to falling off to sleep. I sensed that she was awake, restless and upset. I asked her, 'What's wrong?' She responded, 'Nothing. It's nothing,' and rolled away from me and pretended to fall asleep. Such behavior, I gather, is common among wives. The next night I posed the same questions and added, firmly but lovingly, that it disturbed me when she refused to confide her feelings in me and feigned sleep. For a few minutes she said nothing, and then she rolled towards me and said, 'They are not bald and I do not trust them.'

"This took me by surprise and I demanded an explanation from her. She began by saying that she had no proof of anything but that her spirit told her things, and she had learned to trust what she heard from her spirit. She said that on two occasions she had heard each of them mutter rather vile oaths when they were frustrated with some simple task. I responded that they were still young in the Lord and that bad habits developed over years were the hardest to overcome. Then she said that twice for Clayton and once for Ross she had sensed that they were looking at her not with the gentlemanly look of admiration that she felt from time to time from some of the older gentlemen in the assembly, but with the lascivious look of a sailor just off a ship. I asked, foolishly I gather, what the difference was. She said quite bluntly that it was something that every woman on earth understood even if no man would ever understand. I again stuck up for their side and reminded her that they were bachelors and that the demon of lust had had a long time to work on their souls, and that it was inevitable that it would occasionally rear its ugly and ungodly head.

"She then said that the store had become dirty and had not been dusted. I argued that she was most certainly wrong. The shelves were spotless. 'Only where you can see,' she cried. 'Behind the books and on the top of the volumes there is more dust and grit than we have ever had before. In the basement, the boxes of unopened books have thick layers of dust and dirt on them.' Now it is common among women to think that no one can keep a place as clean as they would have themselves, and such condemnation of maids, housekeepers, or tenants is quite a usual thing when the lady is no longer directly looking after the premises. I suggested this, as gently as I could. Then she rose up out of bed, kicked back the covers and stood to her feet. She looked back at me and said, 'Neither of them is bald. Three times now, for each of them, I had seen small dabs of shaving soap on their heads. They have used their feigned baldness to forge a friendship with you and it is fraudulent. They are using you and I know not what for. But I do not like it and I do not trust them.'

"This troubled me greatly. I have learned to respect my wife's insights and I know they come from the Lord. Yet I was happier now than I had been in several years. We were financially better off than ever before and I was loath to disturb my prosperous world. I promised to confront them, but I kept finding excuses, including the murder of the Scottish engineers that took place during those days, to postpone doing so. Then on Thursday, October 10th they did not open the store and did not again the following day. Neither did they appear at the usual time to retrieve all of the applications I had written. On Sunday they were not at our worship service and then yesterday, Monday, I went to the Trust office, but the door was shut and locked with a little square of cardboard hammered onto the middle of the panel with a tack. Here it is. You can read it for yourself."

He held up a sheet of cardboard, about the size of a sheet of notepaper. It read in this fashion:

THE BRAIN FEVER
CHARITABLE TRUST
IS DISSOLVED

OCTOBER 9, 1890

I was very disturbed and rushed over to their rooming house. There was no answer when I knocked on the door of their rooms. I asked the landlady if they had been seen, and she said that she had seen neither hide nor hair of them since Wednesday. I told her that I was concerned about them and she took her key and opened the door. The rooms were completely empty except for a number of objects left on the table."

"And what might those have been?" asked Holmes.

The man looked as if he were on the verge of tears. His lower lip began to tremble ever so slightly. With an effort, he regained his composure and said, "On the table was a stack of envelopes containing all of the applications and letters I had written. Every one of them. Not one had been sent anywhere. Beside them were well over one hundred books and other items. They corresponded almost exactly with the items they had sold from my store during the time they were looking after it. The whole business had been a fraud. They had deceived me."

"Yet you suffered no financial damage," countered Holmes. "From what you have told me you were not only in a much better cash position than you had ever been, but you now had all your inventory that you could turn around and sell again. The actions were bizarre but where is the crime? They stole nothing from you. They did not strike you or your wife in any way. They did no damage to your premise that a good dusting would not repair. Why are you here and telling me these things?"

Jabez Darby placed his elbows upon his knees and sunk his bald head into his hands. He slowly shook it back and forth and said, "I know. I know. You are right. There is no crime and I feel like a fool telling you all this. I am sure you think us just a couple of silly religious zealots. But we know. We know! In our hearts we know that something is evil. Yet I cannot explain what it is." He placed his hat back on his bald head and started to rise. "I am very sorry to have bothered you with this. I have wasted your time. I am very sorry."

Holmes reached out and firmly placed his hand on the young man's shoulder, stopping him from getting out of his chair. "You and your wife are no fools, my good man. You are entirely correct. It is undeniably true that something evil this way comes. I believe you. Will you take us at once to your shop? And Watson, might you by chance have your doctor's bag with you? Could you bring it along?"

I nodded and from long experience withheld my questioning of such a strange request.

Jabez looked at Holmes with wondering eyes and then nodded. "Thank you, sir. I am much indebted to you. Please. Come with me."

The three of us walked the few blocks from the hotel to the Telegraph Wharf. Jabez Darby unlocked the door, led us inside and, as evening had started to settle in, lighted a lamp. The store was orderly and spotless. "Take us to your basement," said Holmes. Once there Holmes reached up and ran his long fingers along the top of one of the stacks of cases, and asked me to do the same. Even without looking at my hand I could tell by what I felt that the surfaces were thick with grit and dust.

"Is this your usual arrangement for these cases," asked Holmes.

"No. We usually line the stacked cases up along the walls. They have been moved into the center of the room."

The walls of the room were lined with a wooden wainscoting. Holmes proceeded to strike the right-hand wall with his walking stick. He began at one end of the wall and struck regularly at small intervals. Each knock sounded as one would expect a knock against wood that was laid over brick. But as he reached the middle section, the sound changed and there was a distinctly hollow reverberation coming from the wood. A series of knocks indicated that there was a hole of about two feet round behind the wainscoting.

"Watson, I assume that you have a set of forceps in your bag. Forgive me, Doctor, but it is the only tool I could think of that would do the job and immediately available to us."

28

I opened the bag, withdrew my surgical forceps and used them to pry against the planks of wood. There were gaps between the planks where someone had previously inserted a pry bar. The planks peeled off the wall with little effort.

Behind the wood, there was a hole in the brickwork. The far side was covered by similar heavy planks.

"The adjacent building, Holmes," I began, "is it not the harbor branch of Barings?"

"Exactly, my dear Watson. I will wager that it is now several thousand pounds poorer than it was a few days ago. They must have large shipments of payrolls, bullion and negotiable securities moving in and out from the ships. I am surprised that they have not sounded an alarm yet."

Holmes turned to Jabez Darby and said, "You and your wife were correct in your apprehensions and most responsible in your actions. Please give her my warm regards and my admiration for her gifts of discernment."

"But we failed," he said. "The robbery is done. They have used me treacherously and gotten away with it."

"Now there," Holmes again putting his hand on the man's shoulder. "How difficult do you think it will be for Scotland Yard to track down two bald Americans? They will be apprehended in short order, I assure you. Now please, go home to your wife and children and know that you have played a most important role in the solving of a very devious crime."

"Thank you, sir," he said. He led us back up the stairs and we parted our ways; he to his unusually insightful wife and Holmes and me to the police station. We filed our report with the constable on duty and agreed to come back in the morning when the bank opened and a police inspector would be available.

"Well Holmes," I said as we walked back to our rooms, "how on earth did you deduce that they were robbing a bank and not selling Bibles?"

"Elementary, my dear friend. It was perfectly obvious from the first that the only possible object of this intricate deception must be to get the shop owner out of the way. It was a curious but brilliant way of managing it and no doubt suggested to the scoundrels' minds by their knowledge of Mr. Darby's religious convictions and the absence of his hair. The cost of his stipend at the Trust and the false profits they turned over were nothing to them, as they were playing for thousands. Their willingness to volunteer their services demonstrated that they had some strong motive in securing the situation."

"But how could you guess what the motive was?"

"Had any other woman been involved, I should have suspected a mere vulgar motive. However, Mrs. Darby is quite beyond reproach. There was nothing in the shop of any value, the cases of new Bibles notwithstanding. It must then be something out of the shop. The reference made to the accumulation of dust and grit indicated some sort of chiseling, and where could that possibly have taken place without being immediately discerned but in the basement. Remembering that the shop was adjacent to a bank and sharing a common wall led me to the only possible conclusion. Tapping on the wainscoting was all that was required to tell us where they had been chiseling and removing bricks from the basement wall. Those bald-headed villains put a great deal of effort and planning into their devious scheme, but, in the end, it was not really that much of a challenge to see through it."

"Splendid, Holmes," I exulted. "This case solved. Shall I begin to write it up? Or are there still some loose strings to tie up?"

Holmes stopped his walking and gave me that look that I have learned to dread. Without saying anything, his look accused me of being a hopeless fool.

"No, my friend whom I love but who sometimes disappoints me," he said, in a most controlled voice. "There are no loose strings; there are merely several gaping holes in this case. Two men are dead and we still have no way of linking them to the robbery other than what a court would have to consider to be the superstitious fantasies of a devout female member of an odd religious sect. This is far from over."

Chapter Three

A Wild Goose Chase

In the morning we made our way to the police station. An Inspector Johnson was there to meet us. To Holmes's considerable annoyance he had brought along a reporter and a photographer from the local newspaper.

"Thought it would be good to let our citizens know how we all work together to solve a crime," he said. Holmes said nothing. His scowl said it all.

Our little troop marched into Barings Bank and Inspector Johnson demanded to see the manager immediately. A tall, well-dressed gentleman in his mid-fifties came out of his office. "Good morning, Inspector, gentlemen, and to what do I owe the honor of this visit on an otherwise fine morning?"

"How does it feel," blurted out the reporter, "to know that Baring's Bank has been robbed blind?"

"I'm sure I wouldn't know," the manager replied coolly. "Perhaps you could suggest some way to feel since I have never had that experience?"

"Well, you're about to. When was the last time you looked in your vault? You been cleaned out and you don't even know it?" the reporter said loudly.

"Oh my," the manager said with a touch of sarcasm, "why don't we all go and take a look?"

"Please, sir. If you would be so kind to lead the way," said the inspector. The photographer shouted at us to all stop and turn around so he could get a photograph of our descending into the basement. Except for the reporter we kept on walking.

The manager came to a large, heavy iron gate and selected a key from the ring of them that were attached to his belt.

"Who else has a key to this gate?" asked the Inspector.

"Other than me, the only other key is held by Chubbs. They installed the gates."

"So you're saying that you believe Chubbs could have been an accomplice in this robbery, is that right? Can I quote you on that?" said the reporter.

"You most certainly may," said the manager. "In fact, since Chubbs was the only one to install this gate then perhaps it is I who is their accomplice. You may quote me."

"Huh?" said the reporter.

We passed through yet another heavy gate that the manager likewise unlocked. The reporter did not ask any questions.

The last barrier was a large metal door with a dial on the front of it. "Combination locks are being used by most banks today. We use the same type first used by Tiffany's in New York. If you will excuse me please." He turned his back to us. The inspector stood directly in front of the photographer who tried in vain to get a picture of the manager's fingers on the dial.

The door of the vault was opened and he led us into a small room and he activated the electric light bulb. We stood inside the vault room and tried to accustom our eyes to the poor light. Holmes began to knock on the wooden wall panels. He quickly found the one that sounded hollow and I helped him remove it. It came off with no resistance. It could only have been set in place and not nailed or screwed down since the thieves would have pulled it into place behind them as they made their escape.

Behind the panel, there was the same two-foot diameter hole as we had seen on the other side of the wall. Light from the basement of the bookstore shone through. The photographer pushed his way in front of us and took a picture.

"I regret to inform you, sir," said Holmes, "that your vault has been broken into by some very determined and clever thieves and they have robbed you."

"So Mister Bank Manager," demanded the reporter. "How much did they get? Ten thousand pounds, a hundred thousand? And please don't try to tell me you don't know. Every good bank manager knows how much is in his vault. How much did they get?"

"Let me see," said the manager, rubbing his chin. "Let me see. I would have to say that the total amount, in aggregate, net of any taxes would be somewhat less than a farthing. That's f-a-r-t-h . . ."

"I know how to spell *farthing*," the reporter said as he continued to write.

"I'm terribly sorry," said the manager with refined Oxbridgian sarcasm, "I was not aware that you had been to school."

The reporter kept on writing. Then he stopped. "What do you mean 'less than a farthing'? What's that supposed to mean?"

"A farthing, sir, is the smallest denomination in British currency."

"I know what a farthing is," the reporter shouted adding an oath for good measure. "What you're claiming is that they got nothing.

That's impossible. I can see that the shelves here are bare. You've been completely cleaned out! Don't try to cover it up. Baring's has had a heist."

"I fear I must ask you to explain yourself a little less cryptically to us as well," said Holmes. "You appear to be saying that the thieves took nothing."

"That is precisely what I am saying. They took nothing because there was nothing for them to take. This vault was completely empty. Since the day this branch opened a few months ago not a single farthing has been stored here. Your clever thieves have robbed us of precisely nothing."

"What about your shipments to and from the boats?" asked the inspector.

"Nothing remains in this branch overnight. All deposits are kept under heavy guard in the safe upstairs and are loaded onto the London train every evening. They are guarded by no less than four private security men at all times. This vault was built with the intent that someday this branch might be more than a transfer point but so far has never been used. Not for a single farthing. The damaged wall will be repaired in due course, but it appears to have been breached by the world's stupidest bank robbers. They have led you on a chase of a wild goose."

The evening edition of *The Flying Post* had a front-page story under the headline:

World's Stupidest Bank Robbers

Famous London Detective Leads Plymouth Police on "Wild Goose Chase"

The story heaped endless ridicule on Sherlock Holmes. There were several pictures of the bank, the damaged vault, and the group of us who gathered inside of it. The manager was described as "imperious", which I had to admit was true, but since Baring's was a major advertiser, there were no accusations about its lack of a properly secured vault. Fortunately, there was little said about the Darby family, except to present them as a devout couple who had been victims of the ambitious detective from London.

I read the story as we traveled back to London on the same train that must have held the daily bank deposit. Our holiday had been cut short. Holmes said nothing at all and I knew not to attempt to engage him in conversation.

By the time we arrived back at Baker Street in the early hours of the morning a telegram was waiting for us.

Mr. Holmes:

My wife and I are devastated by all
the trouble we have brought upon you.
Words cannot express our apologies. We
know, and heaven knows, that your
intentions were solely for our
protection and the righting of wrong.
Our prayers will continue to be that
the Lord will use this great injustice
to somehow work out His divine plan
and bring the light of truth to shine
upon this dark passage of evil doing.
My wife insists that I add to this
note that while there may be many
words to describe accurately the
criminals who used the names of
Clayton Johns and Ross Duncan,

"stupid" is not one of them. May God
bless you, sir, as He continues to use
you as an instrument of righteousness.

Jabez Nelson Darby

Sherlock Holmes read it and spoke to me for the first time since we had departed the bank. "The lady is absolutely correct, Watson. These men spent nearly a year devising the most elaborate fraud and pulled it off almost perfectly for over two months. They were not fools and, if the good lady is correct, as I am quite sure she is, they had a hand in murder. Yet I cannot deduce the connecting links between their actions, the murders, and the nonsensical bank robbery."

He took the telegram with him and walked slowly towards his bedroom. "Good night, my dear friend. I am sorry that your well-intentioned holiday has been spoiled, and I am grateful for your consideration of my health. Good night."

"Good night, Holmes," I said and made my way home, with a heavy heart.

I did not call in on Sherlock Holmes for several weeks, and when I did one Sunday morning, he failed to answer his door. Mrs. Hudson kindly let me in and I found my friend lapsed into the dull stupor that he used his syringe to inflict upon himself during those times when he required his searing intelligence to cease its operations. He sat in his chair, staring out his window. His eyes were glazed over and a somewhat foolish smile was pasted across his face. I was deeply distressed. I had feared that the events in Plymouth would have this effect on him, and indeed, they had.

On his table was an unopened letter, dated the previous day. The return address indicated that it had been sent by the Little Flock Christian Book Store in Plymouth. It had been addressed both to Mr.

Sherlock Holmes and Dr. John Watson and I took the liberty of opening it and reading it. As soon as I had finished it I laid it down and called for Mrs. Hudson.

"My dear lady, would you be so kind as to bring Mr. Holmes the strongest cup of coffee you are capable of brewing. Something that would induce heartburn in a Turk would be quite in order."

Mrs. Hudson looked at Sherlock Holmes. He gave her a silly smile in return. She then looked at me with a knowing nod and said, "I will fix a brew that will give him a strong jolt back to from Nirvana." Yet again I marveled at her loyalty.

It took some rather unpleasant barking of orders on my part to get Holmes to drink the brew but after an hour, it appeared to have had the desired effect. I then sternly told him to pay attention as I read the letter to him.

Mr. Holmes and Dr. Watson:

I hesitate to make contact with you knowing how terribly our last time together ended. Again we can only thank you for everything you did on our behalf and assure you of our fervent prayers on yours.

I write again at the insistence of my most virtuous wife, whose worth is far above rubies. Neither of us has slept well these past several weeks and last night, at near to three o'clock, she woke me and said, "That man is part of it. I know he is. God has just revealed that to me." As I was only partly awake and entirely confused, I asked "What man?"

She replied, "That evil man who came by the new shop months ago. You must remember him. You must remember how I felt about him."

I did remember. In the early days of the previous summer, just after we had signed our lease on the new property and opened our doors, an unknown man walked into our shop. He was exceptionally well-dressed, with a fine silk hat and walking stick. He was around fifty years of age and greeted us in the most refined manner. He seemed surprisingly well-acquainted with our books and with the Plymouth Brethren movement and he asked many insightful questions of us. As I was still in the depths of my bout of brain fever, I welcomed the distraction he brought to my gloom. I was most impressed with him and began to enjoy our conversation. My wife, who normally is most eager to engage with learned visitors, said nothing. As he departed, he asked if I could tell him about the new building and show him around it, as he was considering recommending it to one of his associates.

I took him outside and we walked around the entire structure. I pointed out the various merchants. Not all had fully set up their operations. He noted that the front section alone had been let out to merchants and that the back portion had only a few unmarked doors. I explained that the entire west side of the building had been leased by the Western Union Telegraph Company since this new building was the terminus of their transatlantic cable from New York, and that the back part held their many switches and rotors and whatever else was required to handle all the thousands of signals that would be received there, processed, and then sent on to London, or Paris, or other parts of the Continent.

As my shop was immediately adjacent to the Western Union office, he expressed concern that the activity and noise might be a problem to the atmosphere of a Christian bookstore, and he seemed genuinely concerned for our operations. I explained that a good thick masonry wall separated my shop from Western Union's operations and that much of the noisy machinery was in their basement and would not disturb us.

He asked if I would mind walking with him back to the Hotel – the same one in which I met with you – as he was not entirely sure of the way. I agreed and we chatted pleasantly about the doctrine of the Rapture, and the priesthood of all believers, and other such topics that are significant to our assemblies.

The route took us through a rather dodgy street alongside the harbor that is known to be the denizen of rough men. From time to time I have met such types in Plymouth and when they accost me and demand money I smile and quote the words of the Apostle Peter to them and I say, 'Silver and gold have I none, but such as I have, give I thee' whereupon I reach into my wallet and bring out a gospel tract and begin to show them the *Romans Road* to salvation. Not one of them has yet converted and been saved by my testimony, but I have been saved many times as they invariably roll their eyes, mutter a few curses, and leave me alone.

Two such men accosted my visitor and me, and I was about to respond in my usual fashion. He, however, made as if he were reaching into his wallet but then in a flurry of actions let fly with a left hook to the face of the one man and brought a dagger down on the extended wrist of the other. The first man grabbed his eye and I could see blood gushing from it. The second had his wrist firmly grasped and his arm twisted so forcefully behind him that I could hear his shoulder become dislocated. He screamed in horrific pain while his accomplice ran off in a panic with blood pouring from his face. The man, my visitor, forced the would-be thief to the sidewalk, placed his face right close and said to him, "Look at me, and remember this face. And do not ever attempt to rob me again or you and your entire family will die in miserable pain. Do you see me? Do you understand me?"

The ruffian had a look of terror upon him and as soon as he was released he ran away. The man composed himself and smiled at me and said, "I did a stint in the Royal Marines when I was young and they trained us to handle situations like this. Some things it has been wise not to have forgotten."

I have known several marines over the years and indeed a few have become part of our assembly of believers. They have all been highly trained, but I have never witnessed from any of them the violence and viciousness that I saw that day. But the man chatted on as if nothing had happened. We parted at the Hotel. He wished me great success and most graciously thanked me for my time. I returned to my shop and my wife.

Upon entering my shop, I heard my wife give a sharp cry and she ran towards me and threw her arms around me. She was sobbing violently. "Oh thank God, thank God" was all she could say and she kept saying it over and over. I had never seen her so sore distraught. It was a full five minutes before she calmed herself and was able to speak to me.

"I do not know who that man was," she said, "but he is as close to the devil himself as I could ever have imagined. The moment he walked in the door, I knew that he was evil. Did you not feel it? Could you not tell?" I confessed that I could not.

"He is a monster, whoever he is. You must promise me that you will never, never, have anything to do with him again. Never. I have been praying the shed blood of the Lord over you since you walked out of the door with him. I have never been so frightened. Promise me that you will have nothing whatsoever to do with him, ever."

My wife, sir, as you witnessed, is a very level-headed woman and I had never seen her so overcome with terror. Fortunately, the day ended and we have never heard from or seen that

man again. We did not even speak of
him until last night when my wife
awoke, convinced that he was somehow
connected with this whole evil
business.

I know not if my sharing this
experience with you will be of any
use. It is my prayer that it would.
About the man himself: he is extremely
tall and thin. His forehead domed out
in a white curve, and his two eyes
were deeply sunken in his head. He was
clean-shaven, pale and ascetic-
looking. I can only remember that he
had no card with him but said that his
name was James Morrison and that he
was a professor of something at
Cambridge.

It is our hope and prayer that this
additional information may be of some
use to you. May God bless and protect
you always,

Jabez Nelson Darby

I finished reading the letter and looked up at Holmes. The silly look of drugged stupor had vanished from his face. The look I expected to see, the look of brilliant and determined concentration and blazing eyes was also not present. What I saw in Holmes's eyes was something I had never seen in all the years I had known him. What I saw was fear.

Holmes rose to his feet and began to pace back and forth across the room in vivid distress.

"Dear God. Oh dear God. He was there. We were right in his lair. Dear God, Watson. I had not expected this. That monster has laid out some terrible plot and we have walked into it by fate. That lovely family in Plymouth will be completely exterminated in the near future. Dear God, Watson."

"Holmes," I cried, "what are you talking about? Who is this man? I have never seen you in such distress. What is it, my friend, what is it?"

With a visible effort, he asserted control over his emotions and fears and quietly sat down in front of me.

"You have probably never heard of Professor Moriarty?" said he.

"Never."

"He is the Napoleon of crime, Watson. He is the organizer of half that is evil and of nearly all that is undetected in this country. He is a genius. He sits motionless, like a spider in the center of its web, but that web has a thousand radiations, and he knows well every quiver of each of them. He is the central power which uses the agent but is himself never caught — never so much as suspected. This is the organization which I alluded to as we traveled to Plymouth, Watson, and to which I now must devote my whole energy to exposing and destroying."

He leaned forward in his chair and looked directly into my eyes. "My dearest friend, you have never failed to support and care for me and I cannot thank you enough. The mystery in which I am now engaged is exceedingly dangerous and it is quite probable that both of us may be killed if we fail to stop this villain. I wish you to have no feelings whatsoever of obligation towards me. I do not expect you to accompany me any further. For the sake of yourself, your wife and the children you yet look forward to having, you are free to walk away and let me continue on my own. I will not love you any the less for doing so."

Sherlock Holmes is not moved to express feelings of the heart and has always spoken of them as weaknesses that have no place in the life of a man of science. Yet here he was affirming the intensity of our friendship in words that I never expected to hear from him.

I rose and affected a casual response. "Shall we meet on the platform of Paddington in an hour? I believe that I am at least entitled to pack my bags and obtain my service revolver before we catch the next train to Plymouth."

His somber look fled and he beamed a smile back at me. "My dear Watson, what's the rush? You may have a luxurious four hours. Forgive me for delaying you but I really must send off a few telegrams before we leave. Such data as we now have before us suggests that Professor Moriarty's interest was not in the bank at all, but in the telegraph office, and I must learn more about it."

We met at Paddington and took our seats in the front carriage. As *The Flying Dutchman* pulled away from the station, Holmes took out a handful of telegrams from his valise.

"Do not just sit there Holmes," I chided. "What have you learned?"

"The Plymouth Brethren sect claims to be free of all denominational administration, but they appear to know everything about every one of their locals churches from Auckland to Halifax. I contacted one of the Brethren that fellowships at a Gospel Hall in the West End and he provided me with the contact information for the Assembly of Believers Meeting on Union Street in Brooklyn, the local church which was claimed by Messrs Johns and Duncan to have been their sponsoring assembly. They confirmed that yes indeed they had commended two young Christians to the mission work in the Faroe Islands and that their names were Ross Duncan and Clayton Johns."

"So that part is true," I asked.

"No, that part is just further evidence of the extent that Moriarty and his ilk have gone to in setting up this crime. The good folks in

Brooklyn also informed me that their men were already in the Faroes, had cashed the wire transfers of financial support that were sent, and most certainly have never been bald. Our two bank robbers assumed their identities as part of the pretense.

"But they also added that last year two other men had attended many of their services and had aroused some suspicion, particularly among the wives. These men gave their names as Isaac Proctor and Anthony Pistone. They had been most inquisitive about the beliefs and practices of the Brethren and asked innumerable questions but never took part in the Lord's Supper service that is restricted to confirmed believers. They had no visible means of support at the time but had ready access to all the funds they needed to live comfortably. Their idle chit chat with the church members led some to assume that they had worked in the telegraph business as they seemed to have quite extensive knowledge about its operations. I deduced that these two men were recruited by Moriarty and assumed the identities of the two missionaries.

"A late telegram to the personnel office of Western Union confirmed that men by these names had been previous employees of Western Union in America, had been highly skilled engineers, and had abruptly quit their employment in the summer of last year.

"The Office of the Public Trustee wired back that there was no such charity as *Here Today, Gone Tomorrow*, or some name like that. Our scoundrels fabricated that as well.

"I also sent a note to the Western Union office here in London. I had a prompt reply from the manager, a Colonel Thomas Sutherland. He was terribly disturbed by the murder of those two men who were working for him and has insisted on coming to Plymouth to speak with us and try to help. I had informed him that I was quite sure that some sort of scheme had been perpetrated upon their operations. He will join us and is bringing his head communications engineer with him."

"I spoke finally with Inspector Lestrade. He was quite up on the murders and welcomed my looking into them. He was not free to come himself but agreed to send one of his official agents, Peter Jones. You may remember him. He is an absolute imbecile in his profession, but he is as brave as a bulldog and as tenacious as a lobster if he gets his claws upon anyone."

"This is all very well, Holmes," I said. "But other than the murders for which you still have no clear motive, what crime was committed? What are we looking for?"

Holmes sighed, "My friend, I simply do not know. All the data I have has convinced me that Moriarty is behind this and that he has spent well over a year planning it, down to the smallest detail. As a result, I know beyond a shadow of a doubt that there is a very monstrous crime involved and that it will yield great ill-gotten gain to Moriarty and his syndicate. I am reasonably certain it is closely tied to the telegraph services of Western Union, but I do not yet know what it could possibly be that they have done, or are doing, or are about to do. That is what I hope to discover. And I am also very sure that once Moriarty learns that we are on his trail, he will take ruthless steps to stop us."

With this Holmes lapsed back into his near-trance of concentration. I read and re-read the telegrams and the letters from Mr. and Mrs. Darby and tried my best to see anything in them that Holmes had not, but after two hours I had to admit that I also failed to see anything new. We had victims of a crime, but we had no motive, and we did not even know what the crime had been.

Chapter Four

Arbitrage

We pulled into Millbay Station by the end of the day and made our way back to the Duke of Cornwall. The excellent chefs at the grand hotel provided us with a tasty supper, after which we rose to go to what I hoped would be a decent night's sleep.

"The chaps from Western Union and the man from Scotland Yard have agreed to meet up with us over breakfast," said Holmes. "Until the morrow, my good Doctor."

I came down early for breakfast. Holmes was already seated at the table. I noticed that there were six places set. "Is someone else joining us, Holmes?" I asked.

"Perhaps. I told the kitchen there might be one more. It does not matter."

Within a few more minutes Agent Jones had appeared and renewed his acquaintance with Holmes and me. Two other men approached the table. The older one, dressed in an American style business suit with a short jacket and long necktie, introduced himself to us, speaking the accent of a gentleman of The South. "Gentlemen, my name is Thomas Sutherland the Third, from Western Union in America, and I am in charge of our operations here in Europe. This here's my chief engineer, Donald Macquarrie. He's from Glasgow he talks kind of peculiar, but he's just as smart as a whip and we're powerful glad you all are taking an interest this tragedy. Right fine of you. Much appreciated."

As he and the young Scotsman seated themselves, a woman walked purposefully up to the table and sat down at the extra place. She was tall, broad-shouldered with a full head of red hair, and dressed smartly if modestly. "Good morning, gentlemen," she said. "I am Mrs. Jabez Darby and since Doctor Watson cannot be involved at one and the same time in apprehending criminals as well as being recording secretary for Sherlock Holmes I am taking over the secretarial tasks. I would not usually offer to work on the Sabbath, but matters cannot be helped. Is that not correct, Mr. Holmes?" she said with the confidence of a woman who is used to being right, and before the men could stand up to greet her took her place at the remaining table setting.

Sherlock Holmes looked intently at his new secretary, and even he could not conceal the traces of a smile at the corner of his mouth. "That is quite correct, Mrs. Darby, and now gentlemen and lady, let us get on with the matters at hand. Colonel Sutherland, we strongly suspect that there is something in the Western Union building that is the object of a criminal syndicate but we as yet do not know what it is. Could you please inform us about the structure and function of that office?"

"Sure. I can do that," said the Colonel with a deep voice and refined Southern cadence. "The Western Union Company is the world greatest provider of telegraph services. We now have well over a million miles of cables stretching around the earth and across every continent, except, of course, for the Antarctic, but when the day comes that the penguins need a telegraph cable, we'll just get one to them too."

"Of course," said Holmes, "but as we are in Plymouth and not in the Antarctic, perhaps you could restrict your information to our immediate location."

"Sure. I can do that. In 1865 our company invented and gave America the world first stock ticker machine."

"Don't you mean to say 1869," said Mrs. Darby, as she continued, using rapid shorthand, to take down every word spoken. "Your 1865 model was only a prototype. It did not appear on the floor of the New York Stock Exchange until 1869."

She said this in a matter-of-fact tone of voice that took the Colonel off-guard. He stared at her for a moment and seeing that she meant no offense nodded in a gentlemanly way and continued. "Right you are, Ma'am. Right you are. As I am sure you folks know, we have hundreds of wonderful companies in America, and many of them are public stock companies, and are traded on the various stock exchanges of the world. Not to make you English boys feel second fiddle or anything like that, but the stock exchange in London is the second largest now after New York. Kind of a distant second, but second nonetheless, and still a real important place. So we all decided over a decade ago that we needed to have one of our stock ticker units right there, right in the middle of your London Stock Exchange, so your firms could do the type of real fast up-to-the-minute trading that we've become accustomed to in New York City.

"Now, in order for that to happen, we decided that we needed our very own transatlantic telegraph cable that would run without interference from New York City to merry old England. So we strung one all the way across the ocean. Now most of the other cable fellows, they ran their cables from Nova Scotia or Newfoundland and ended up in Skewjack down by your Land's End. But that place was getting kind of crowded so we chose to go a few hundred miles more and run straight as a rifle shot from Long Island all the way to Plymouth, and then we could just follow the railway line right into what you folks call The City. And that cable is now up and running and working just fine and dedicated only to business. No happy birthday greetings or any of that family stuff, just business.

"That cable arrives at our new building on your Telegraph Wharf here in Plymouth and there we splice it up, boost it up, and send one branch line back over to Dover and on to Paris. A second and a third run cross-country then across the Channel to Amsterdam and Berlin, and then we run smaller branches back over to the Irish in Dublin and up to the Scots in Edinburgh. At two-thirty every afternoon — well now, that would be three-thirty on the Continent — all the opening prices from Wall Street come flooding through our cables. And that way everybody in Europe gets what's happening in New York at exactly the same time and so they can all do trades at the same time as we do in our Wall Street and everything is fair and square. And that's what our building here is for. Isn't that right, Donny? Did I miss anything?" he said, looking over at his chief engineer.

"No sir. I believe you covered it all," said the Scotsman.

"Please tell us about these two men who were murdered," said Holmes.

"Well sir, I have had just two days in my life that I consider to have been the worst that I could imagine. The first was the ninth of April in the year of Our Lord, 1865. I don't suppose you English fellows know what took place on that terrible day?"

None of the other four men spoke up. Without lifting her head from her note-taking, Mrs. Darby said, "I believe that was the day when, having lost to the Northern Yankees, the Southern Rebels were forced to surrender at Appomattox and give up their slaves." She continued to make notes oblivious to the glare she was receiving from the Colonel. Ever the gentleman, he smiled courteously and said, "Well I suppose your facts are accurate even if we might not share the same perspective on them. The second worst day of my life was just a few weeks ago when two har-working young men were murdered just a couple of blocks from where we now sit. They were good family men with devoted wives and lovely children. I had hoped against hope that the police would come up with some reason other than their doing work for Western Union to explain why they were murdered, but there has been none. They got themselves killed just because they were doing a job that I had ordered and Donny here had designed. We have done everything we could for their families and they won't ever be in want, but their deaths are a very heavy burden on my heart."

I did not doubt his sincerity or the depth of his feelings. He ceased speaking and extracted his handkerchief from his pocket and wiped tears away from both eyes. "I am sorry gentlemen . . . and lady, but that was a very hard day for all of us and our being here today is because that event is far from over. We need to get to the bottom of this. And I would be most grateful if we can all somehow work together to get there."

"I hope so as well," said Holmes, "and could you please continue and tell us what these men were doing for you?"

The Colonel nodded. "These two men were independent engineers and had their own consulting firm somewhere in Scotland."

"In Glasgow, sir," said Donald.

"Right, in Glasgow. Well, they bid on the contract to do all the installation of the wiring and switching that I talked about earlier. And they gave a good bid, and had real good references, so we gave them the contract, and they came here and did it all. And they did real fine work, did they not, Donny?"

"Yes, sir. Their work was quite brilliant."

"It was the next to last day, the day when they had soldered in the last coupling of the secondary cables. The following day was to be the final inspection. Then we all were going to gather in the office and have a little celebration and bid them farewell, our employees having become rather fond of them. They went walking back to their rooming house and somebody shot them. Nobody heard the shot, but the autopsy said that someone must have put a revolver right close to their heads. Is that not right, Mr. Policeman?"

"Yes, sir. That is what I read as well in the reports," said Agent Jones.

"Thank you, Colonel Sutherland. May I suggest that we all now make our way to Telegraph Wharf," said Holmes. "It would be good if each of us could look at both the basement of the bookstore and the interior of the Western Union installation. There is something amiss somewhere and I believe that if we can find what has been done it should bring us closer to the killers and the reasons for the murder."

We made our way from the hotel over to the wharf and entered the bookstore. Jabez Darby led us down to the basement. I noticed that the dust and grime had all been cleaned away from the tops of the cases. Holmes repeated the task he had done a few weeks earlier but instead of knocking on the wooden panels of the right, he went up and down the wall on the left side of the basement. Again we heard the distinct sound of a hollow section behind a panel and he motioned to me. This time, I was prepared and had brought along a proper pry bar and I quickly removed the panels. Behind them, as Holmes had deduced, was another hole in the masonry, but rather larger than the one on the left that had so completely tricked us.

"Mr. Macquarrie," said Holmes, "addressing the Scottish engineer, "as you are the youngest and most limber of the lot of us, may I prevail upon you to crawl inside this hole and give a good push to whatever you find on the far side of it?"

The engineer got down on his hands and knees and moved his body into the hole. We heard a loud crash as panels on the other side fell into the basement room of Western Union."

"Thank you, sir, thank you," said Holmes. "We shall meet up with you on the other side of this wall in just a few minutes."

And so we did. After fetching Mr. Macquarrie out of the hole, the Colonel gave us a guided tour of the installation. It was rather impressive to a novice technician such as I. It was equipped with both steam tubes and electrical wires. There were many gleaming new machines humming, and clicking, and banging, and clanking. A team of workmen in overalls was tending to them, making sure that they were all oiled and kept in perfect running order. Donald Macquarrie had brought with him a roll of blueprints and he was looking at each unit as we passed, comparing it to what was shown on the drawings.

"They have been here, and they have changed something," said Holmes. "It may take us some time, but we must find out what they have done."

We began at the corner where the massive cable from the Atlantic Ocean entered the building. One by one we moved past the various machines following the path of the current. At each machine, the engineer compared what he saw on his blueprints to what existed in the reality of the building. Each time he shook his head and said, "No gentlemen. There is nothing amiss here. All according to plan."

We were approaching the far corner of the building where the cable was spliced before being run off to the various exchanges of Great Britain and Europe, and I began to worry that we might be yet again on a wild goose chase. The engineer stopped and looked at the Colonel. "Sir, I believe you said that we had auxiliary cables running to Amsterdam, Berlin, Paris, Dublin, Edinburgh, and London."

"That's right," affirmed the Colonel.

"Sir, that is only six stock exchanges. Are you sure that we are not serving any other locations?"

"Impossible. Those are our only offices. You know that, Donny. Why are you asking?"

"Because sir, there are eight auxiliary cables branching off of the main one and not six."

"That's plum crazy," said the Colonel. "Let me see."

Like a child counting toy blocks, the Colonel placed his hand on one auxiliary cable after the other, each separated by about eighteen inches as it was spliced off the main cable. "One . . . two . . . three . . . four. . . Yup. There's eight. Check these out will you, Donny. Are all of these wires real and working?"

The engineer removed a small instrument from his tool case. I recognized it as a recently patented current sensor with two protruding wires, both connected to a small electric bulb. He placed the ends of the wires on each of the auxiliary cables in turn. Each time the bulb glowed. "They're all live, sir. It may take us a few hours, but we can have our men follow each one of them after they leave the building and find out where they lead. Two of them have to be going someplace we don't know about. It looks as if someone is stealing our signals."

"Right. Get that done right away, Donny. And then rip out whichever of those cables isn't ours. We'll have those pirates put out of business in no time."

"May I suggest, sir," said Holmes, "that you might be much more helpful to the apprehending of those who murdered your men if you were not to do that quite so quickly."

"What do you mean?" asked the Colonel.

"Mr. Macquarrie, sir," said Holmes, "could I impose on you to use your sensor to test the main cable at each of the intervals between the auxiliary cables beginning at the far end?

"There has to be current all the way through the main cable, sir," replied the engineer, "otherwise the far auxiliary ones couldn't light up, and they all did."

"Nevertheless," said Holmes, "would you mind doing that for me? It can only take a moment."

The engineer shrugged his shoulders and placed his instrument on the sections of the main cable between each of the auxiliary cables. He began at the far end and, as expected, the current sensor lit up each time. The section between auxiliary cables seven and eight was alive, as was the section between six and seven, and on down the line.

The section of the main cable between auxiliaries one and two was dead. The sensor failed to glow.

The engineer immediately took his sensor away and looked closely at it. Then he tested it again on other sections and again it glowed. He returned to the portion of the main cable that showed no current. Again there was no reaction from the sensor.

"That's impossible!" said the engineer. "There cannot possibly be a part of the main cable that has no current otherwise the rest of it would all be dead. This is madness."

"No, my good man, it is not madness," said Holmes. "It is diabolical ingenuity. The only possible explanation for what you have just discovered with your current sensor is that auxiliary cables one and two are not auxiliary at all. They are nothing less than the main cable and form a detour loop. And I will assure you, sir, that somewhere along that loop someone is reading all your stock price information before sending it along to the exchanges."

"Why would they want to do that, Mr. Holmes?" asked the police agent. "It is an invasion of privacy, but it hardly constitutes a major crime and certainly nothing that might motivate a murder."

"It's arbitrage fraud and they stand to make millions of pounds every month," said Mrs. Darby.

"Pardon me, ma'am," said the Colonel. "But I am afraid I do not understand you."

The lady hesitated to answer but, after receiving a nod from Holmes, proceeded. "There have been several articles in *The Times* about it over the past few years, sir. This is how it works. Let us suppose that a shrewd financial investor were able to see the price of a stock, shall we say Imperial Oil, on both the New York and the Chicago stock exchanges at the very same time, and he observed that the New York price had just shot up by five and seven-eighths but that the Chicago price had not yet moved. What might he send in an immediate telegram to his broker in Chicago?"

"Well for sure he would tell him to buy a whole bunch of shares real fast because the price was for sure going up by a whole lot."

"Exactly sir. And that is what the traders call arbitrage. If I understand Mr. Holmes, he is suspecting that these villains have set up a scheme by which they can do that fraudulently. Is that correct, Mr. Holmes?"

"Correct," replied Holmes. "I will wager, Colonel Sutherland, that most of your messages about the opening prices on the New York Stock Exchange arrive in a timely manner, but that a select few of them are mysteriously delayed, arriving fifteen to thirty minutes late."

"How could they do that," queried the police agent.

"I would suspect," continued Holmes, "that somewhere not far away from here, and most likely quite close to the General Post and Telegraph Office, they have set up one of your stock ticker machines, with a teleprinter attached. They just remove their stock of choice until they have had an opportunity to send a wire to their broker, buy some shares, and then let the rest of the world catch up with them."

"But that's not like robbing a bank," said the Agent. "Where's the money in that?"

"Thousands of pounds every single day," said Mrs. Darby. "They can buy knowing that a stock is sure to rise, or they can short it, knowing that it is sure to fall. They would only have to trade a small handful of stocks every day to make a fortune, and, if I am not correct, Mr. Holmes, the people they rob do not even know that they have been swindled, and it is all done without having to fire a shot, or rob a bank."

"Robbing a bank is what they pretended to do," said Holmes. "And indeed, they fooled us and have, without a doubt, garnered several thousand pounds for their efforts already."

"Then why is it, sir, that you do not want us to put those varmints out of business right away?" asked the Colonel.

"Ah, because," said Holmes, his eyes sparkling, "because I believe that we can best them at their own game, do some rather nasty damage to their financial health, and entice them into our trap."

Chapter Five

The Noisy Nothing

The following morning was Monday and I ate breakfast alone at the hotel. Holmes had been up and out very early and had left a note for me asking that I join him at the bookstore around one o'clock in the afternoon. I did so and found the shop to be a hive of activity. The front room where the books and tracts were displayed was untouched, but the back office had been transformed. There were now two stock ticker machines, two teleprinters, and a web of wires and cables running back and forth every which way. Mr. Macquarrie, the engineer, and several of his men were scurrying to and fro with great energy.

I shuffled into the basement and observed another two workers huffing and puffing as they man-handled a strange looking machine through the still gaping hole in the right-hand wall and into the vault of the bank. They had also run a steam hose and an electrical cable from the Western Union cellar, clear across the cellar of the bookstore and into the vault.

"Come, Watson, the game is afoot," shouted Holmes from the top of the stairs.

"Good heavens, Holmes," I shouted back to him as I climbed back up. "What havoc are you wreaking on this gentle bookstore?"

Holmes, uncharacteristically standing without his suit coat, and with his shirtsleeves rolled part-way up, smiled, "We are going to hoist that villain Moriarty on his own petard. And if we cannot put him away, we will do very nasty damage to his bank account."

"He is not going to be very happy, Holmes," I said with a smile at my devious friend, but had no idea how he intended to accomplish his plans.

"He will not be happy at all Watson, not at all. And that is the second part of our intrigue. I fully suspect that within a few days we will have an unfriendly visit from his henchmen, if not from the evil genius himself. He will be going mad wanting to know what has gone wrong. And we shall be lying in wait for them to come to us and enter our trap."

"And just where is this trap of yours, Holmes?"

"Why in the vault of the bank, of course. Our very industrious accomplice, Mr. Macquarrie, has adapted one of their machines and now it makes all sorts of wondrous clacking and banging and ringing sounds as it lights up and spits out printed tapes. It whistles and whirs and hums like no machine you have ever seen before. It will be inside the vault and will surely entice them to join it."

"But what does it *do* Holmes?" I had to ask.

"Oh, that's quite elementary, my dear friend. It does absolutely nothing. It will do naught but sit inside the vault and make all sorts of loud sounds and flashes. And we will just have to watch what happens next."

I knew better than to ask, although my curiosity was on fire. I had to be content to sit down beside Mrs. Darby and the Colonel, who were peering over the latest *Financial Times* and having quite the spirited conversation about the prospects of American companies that were listed on both the New York and London Stock Exchanges.

"Your Mr. Holmes has requested," Mrs. Darby said in response to my asking her what they were doing, "that we become familiar with those stocks that are considered volatile, ones that could quite reasonably either move up or down sharply on any given day. So we are familiarizing ourselves with their history and prospects."

"And, I might add," said the Colonel, "having just a real good time doing so. This here is a very well-informed young woman and I do believe she and I have missed our calling. We would of been smarter, the both of us, to do this for a living rather than selling Bibles and managing telegraphs. Do you not agree, Mrs. Darby?"

She laughed. "I never knew I had any such talent. I do not recall from my study of the scriptures that God gave insight into financial markets as one of the spiritual gifts. And I am quite certain that there is no such thing in all of the Bible, or in the entire history of the Church, called a *dead cat bounce.*"

A what!?" I stammered.

She and the Colonel both laughed. "Well now, Doctor," said the Colonel, "that's just an all-American way of describing a stock that used to be high and got low real fast and then looked as if it were coming back up. We call it that because when you drop anything from a high enough spot, even a dead cat, well, it's just going to bounce. So I was explaining that this here Electro-Steam Company of Pennsylvania only looks like it's going back up. But it ain't going anywheres but right back down. It ain't no better than a dead cat."

I smiled at the two of them. "But why are you doing this? Did Holmes explain what he was going to do with all your efforts?"

Both of them looked a little sheepish. "Well, now, sir, we got to admit that he wasn't all that clear. Maybe you can help us with that one. Is it us or does he sometimes not lay all his cards on the table? We're just not real sure what he has in mind. You got some idea?"

I sighed. "No, my friends. But I have lived with him long enough to be sure that he has his reasons that our lesser reason knows not of."

By two o'clock in the afternoon, everything appeared to be in place. Sherlock Holmes called our little troop together and warmly told us that he had christened us as the newest members of his Company of Irregulars. The Colonel, Mr. and Mrs. Darby, Mr. Macquarrie, and Police Agent Peter Jones were all quite pleased with his so doing. I did not have the heart to tell them that their senior officers in the Company were the urchins of Baker Street.

"We have had some useful data from Inspector Lestrade," said Holmes. "He has made inquiries at the London Stock Exchange and there has been some unusual trading going on there over the past few weeks. A certain Zurich Investments Company, a rather secretive firm out of Switzerland, has had a very lucky streak. They have made some large and bold trades on American stocks every day between two thirty and four thirty in the afternoon and regardless of whether they are buying or shorting, their trades are paying off handsomely."

"So that is Moriarty's syndicate?" I asked.

"You may be sure of it," replied Holmes. "And, if our little troop can perform cleverly on the field of battle, the syndicate is about to become distinctly impoverished."

We sat quietly in the back office of the Little Flock Bookstore watching the silent stock ticker machines. At a few seconds past two-thirty in the afternoon, at the same time as the exchanges opened in New York City, they sprang to life. There was a humming and clicking, and banging sound and the printed ticker tapes started to fly out of them. The Colonel was manning one and Mrs. Darby the other. They called out the results as they appeared.

"Dunlop Rubber down an eighth," announced the Colonel.

"Provident Financial up one and three-eighths," read Mrs. Darby, "But it trades at over one hundred dollars a share, so that is not much of a change."

And on they went reading the tapes. "Cable Piano down an eighth, Oneida up a quarter, Paine Webber down a quarter."

Then Mrs. Darby let out a short "Aha!" We looked at her and she announced, "Colorado Coal up three and a quarter. That's a jump of nearly twenty percent."

"Excellent," said Holmes as he rubbed his hands together. "Mr. Darby, please send it down by three and a quarter instead." Jabez Darby, on the teleprinter machine, typed in the instructions.

"Here's another!" called out the Colonel. "Carter's Little Liver Pills is down by two. They were trading at twelve. So that's quite the drop."

"Do you think," I asked, "that the American public finally woke up and stopped buying snake oil?"

"Sorry Doc," the Colonel rebuked me. "Those are just the greatest thing to come along. My Aunt Bessy swears by them. They aren't going out of business for a long time."

"Very well," interrupted Holmes, "the history of the medicinal choices of the American public is a monument to the resilience of the physical constitution of the average citizen. But that is none of our affair. Mr. Macquarrie, could you please send that stock up by two instead."

"Right sir. Done sir," said the engineer as he typed into his machine.

"Have any of you ever heard of something called *Coca-Cola?*" Mrs. Darby shouted to the group of us. "Their stock just keeps going up."

"It's a new tonic, a genuine elixir concocted a couple of years back by a real fine Southern pharmacist," said the Colonel. "Let the professor think it's going down and short it, 'cuz it ain't never going down. It's the real thing."

Professor Moriarty would soon be shorting Coca-Cola.

We kept up the intense pace for a full two hours and then Holmes abruptly called a stop. "It is four thirty and the Exchange has closed for the day. We shall return tomorrow and make more mischief for the professor." With this, we said our good-byes for the day and went to our several abodes. As Holmes sat down to dinner in the hotel, he looked positively gleeful. "Tut, tut, Holmes," I upbraided him. "We mustn't become over-confident."

"You are quite correct, Watson," he responded. "But so far it is all going swimmingly, is it not?"

"I am sure I would agree with you if I had any true understanding of what it is you have us doing."

"Ah, that will all become clear in a very short time. For now, you must trust me and be sure that we have turned the tables on scoundrels and are hurting them where they do not like to be hurt.

"For the rest of the evening perhaps I will go and enjoy the beauty of Nature looking over the seacoast. What do you say to that, Watson?"

"I would say you are either going mad or are annoyed with yourself that you forgot to bring your violin or any books along. You have no use or appreciation for Nature whatsoever."

"Oh my, you do know me far too well my friend. You are right, but the promenade along the coast is as good a place for a three pipe concentration as any in this provincial city and the good lady forbids me to smoke in our battle office. So allow me to bid you good evening. The Company of Irregulars assembles tomorrow at two o'clock."

The evening was uneventful, as was the following morning. At two o'clock, again a half hour before the opening of the exchanges in New York, the Irregulars gathered at their posts.

"Our assault on the enemy is working exactly as I had imagined," said Holmes to the members of the Company. "We are inflicting damage on them from which, if we can sustain the attack, they will not recover."

"Well now, that's real good, Mister Holmes," said the Colonel, "but ain't it past time when you explained just what it is we're doing to the enemy? I have been a soldier, sir, and any enemy I did damage to was standing there in front of me, and you'll just have to excuse me, but I just don't happen to be seeing no enemy round about here."

Like a grinning schoolboy showing off his model train set, Holmes explained his battle plan.

"As you have seen, at two-thirty every weekday afternoon the cables from New York City bring across the opening prices of their Exchange. Professor Moriarty devised a brilliant scheme to see the stock prices before anybody else on this side of the pond. He then runs in front of them, buying or shorting, knowing he cannot lose, and he pockets the profits. We are doing the exact same thing to Professor Moriarty. We have only two hours a day while the exchanges in London and New York are open simultaneously, and during which we are altering the stock price he sees. He now runs in front of the stocks and does exactly the wrong thing. He is doing precisely the opposite of what he hoped to do and is losing thousands of pounds within minutes."

In a way that copied the delaying loop that Moriarty had placed in front of the cables to the exchanges, Holmes had Mr. Macquarrie install a short delaying loop in Moriarty's cable. A chosen stock that opened higher on New York would be changed to opening lower, and those that opened down would be shown to Moriarty as having surged upwards. He would rush to buy the stocks that would fall, and to short the stocks that would rise.

"I have a telegram from Inspector Lestrade informing us that, most curiously, the winning streak of the mysterious Swiss firm came to a crashing halt yesterday. Lestrade's contact in the Exchange estimates that the poor dears lost nearly fifty thousand pounds yesterday."

"Bravo," we all cheered. "Right, back to our posts," chipped in the Police Agent, who did not, in fact, have a post, but stood ready to defend us against whatever danger might appear. Our bravado did not fully disguise our sense that our brilliant game could not continue unchallenged for very long.

Chapter Six

The Visitors

Yet the game did continue. Our routine of reading and altering stock prices went on uninterrupted through Tuesday, and again on Wednesday and Thursday. Each day before starting our tasks Holmes read us the telegrams from Lestrade and each day we cheered at the tens of thousands of pounds of financial causalities we had inflicted.

"He cannot let this go on much longer. I am surprised that he has not yet paid us a visit," said Holmes to his Irregulars as we gathered early Friday afternoon.

At four o'clock a boy appeared with a telegram and handed it to Holmes. He read it and looked up at us. "Cease operations, please troops. We are informed that as of twenty minutes ago our enemies have stopped making any trades on the London Exchange. They were being far more greedy than I had thought they would be and, overcome by their early success, had begun to trade on margin. Their creditors became alarmed and have called their loans. The scoundrels are now in debt by nearly one million pounds."

With this news, we broke into spontaneous applause and hoots and hollers. "My friends," said Holmes as his smile changed to a quite serious look, "our time of fun and games is over. We can expect some dangerous visitors before the weekend has passed."

It mattered not. We were elated and celebrated with a supper together at an elegant seafood restaurant. As we parted, Holmes once more admonished us, "We must all remain close to our residences. You may be called upon at any time to return to the bookstore post haste and come prepared for dangerous undertakings. Mr. Darby, I am sure that you do not own a revolver but, Colonel, I am equally sure that you do."

"Sir, the Second Amendment of the Constitution of the United States of America guarantees me that right. It says . . .," and he proceeded to quote it to us. I did not have the heart to remind him that he was in the Mother Country and not in the colony that got away. I fully expected him to show up when called bearing several revolvers and perhaps a Winchester rifle, or two, and silently thanked James Madison for his contribution to the security of a free Christian bookstore.

I retired to bed shortly after midnight. Holmes was still in our shared sitting room and pacing back and forth. I did not expect him to sleep again until this adventure was over.

Although I lay awake for what I was sure was well over an hour I finally fell into a deep sleep. At three-thirty in the early morning, Holmes shook me awake. "Get dressed Watson. They are here," he said urgently. I emerged into our sitting room and saw a young constable waiting for us. "Police Agent Jones," he said, "sent me on the double to tell you, gentlemen, that he had officers watching the station, and on the late train three rather suspicious looking strangers arrived and made their way to a rooming house near the General Post Office. He has several more constables waiting in the allies near Telegraph Wharf, sir. He wanted you to know that. He suggests that you should come at once, sir, if your plan is to work. Otherwise, he can't move against them as they haven't done anything yet."

"Thank you, Constable," Holmes said and gave the young chap a pat on the back. "You have done your job well and we are on our way."

In the darkness, we made our way to the bookstore and assembled our little troop in silence. To my surprise, Mrs. Darby had accompanied her husband. "Madam," I whispered, "this is no place for a woman. These are dangerous men we are dealing with. Mr. Darby, sir, I am shocked that you would permit your wife to be in such a situation."

"Doctor Watson," Mrs. Darby responded in a whisper, "I assure you that I have never, throughout our entire marriage, ever disobeyed my husband's instructions."

Jabez Darby gave me a gentle elbow in the ribs and whispered, "That's because I have never instructed her to do anything I knew she did not want to do. It's an excellent prescription for a happy marriage, Doctor. You might recommend it to your patients." I could detect the two of them restraining their laughter. I was not amused.

"Is your noisy nothing all set to be fired up, Mr. Macquarrie," asked Holmes.

"Aye, it is," the engineer replied. "And proud of it I am, sir."

We resumed our silence and sat in stillness for another hour. At first light, a constable silently entered the office and lowered his head to the police agent. "They're on their way, sir. There's five of them."

"There were only three on the train," countered Agent Jones. "Where did the other two come from?"

"They seem to have met at the rooming house sir," said the constable. "And sir, the other two are rather odd looking chaps."

"In what way?"

"Well sir, they're both bald as babies. Very strange sir."

"Hmm. Thank you, constable. Very well. To our posts," agent Jones whispered to us.

The men made their way down the stairs and into the basement. Mrs. Darby, not entirely pleased with being so, was assigned the post of sentry and would remain in the office. Once in the basement, the engineer worked his way through the hole in the left side wall and into the basement of Western Union. Holmes, the Colonel, Mr. Darby and I each secreted ourselves behind stacked cases marked "Oxford University Press - Scofield Bibles." Each stack had to be well over a hundredweight. Agent Jones stood in a small alcove, with his revolver drawn.

I jumped with a start as the most ungodly noise began from within the bank vault. There were intermittent flashes of light, bangs, and whistles, and clacking and clanging sounds all coming in a great cacophony through the hole in the basement wall.

"Good heavens," I whispered to Holmes, "What in the name of all that is holy is that?"

"He's is a Scot," said Holmes, "and I fear he was a little carried away demonstrating the superiority of Scottish engineers. It truly is the most fearsomely noisy machine I have ever seen, and it does absolutely nothing. I expect it will drive our scoundrels mad."

We said not another word. The light and the noise from the bank vault continued unabated. Some five minutes later we heard a series of quiet taps on the floor just above us. I dared not breathe.

Four men descended the stairs. I gave a nudge to Holmes and held up four fingers, followed by a questioning gesture, and then five fingers. He shrugged and then pointed up and towards the street, followed by raising a hand flat above his eyes, indicating a lookout. I nodded and waited.

Our visitors gathered in the center of the basement, all looking towards the hole in the brick wall from which the sounds and lights were coming. One of them crouched down and attempted to look inside. He cursed, and then he got to his hands and knees and made his way through the hole into the vault. We could hear him shout, "What the . . ." followed by a series of curse words.

A second man, one of the two with the bald heads, also crouched down and crawled into the vault. I could hear some loud banging sounds and I deduced that one of the scoundrels was striking the marvelous machine with his foot. The machine, in response, gave off a very loud whistle. It sounded as if a train were approaching. I smiled, knowing that behind the other wall Mr. Macquarrie had opened the steam hose and let it blast away.

The remaining two men had kept peering into the hole but with the whistle blast jumped back in fright, and then they quickly crawled through as well. "Now!" shouted Holmes, and one after the other we put our shoulders to our stacked cases of Bibles and completely blocked up the hole. Our villains were trapped inside the bank vault.

Again we heard loud cursing and could feel them pushing against the cases, but to no avail. It was not difficult to hold them back with the combined weight of our bodies and the cases. Then came the first revolver shot. I looked at Holmes and he calmly said, "Let them fire away. There is not a revolver ever made that is powerful enough to penetrate four feet of books."

Several more constables who had been watching the street came pounding down the stairs. There were more revolver shots. All were harmlessly absorbed by the books. I turned to Mr. Darby and with as close as I will ever come to gallows humor said, "No doubt we are being protected by the Word of God, but I'm afraid that they will be of little retail value after such a nasty attack upon them."

Mr. Darby, bracing his back against his stack of cases, gave me a thumbs-up signal. "If I can say they were damaged by bullets while protecting believers against evil doers then I shall be able to sell them at a premium. Some of my customers are rather fond of such items."

When the shots had ceased Agent Jones lowered his head towards the edge of the hole, pushed the cases back an inch, and shouted, "I am arresting you on suspicion of bank robbery, you do not have to say anything but it may harm your defense if you do not answer in question something you later rely on in court; anything you do say may be given in evidence. Now then, there are several police officers on the other side of this hole and all are armed. You cannot escape and you have trapped yourself in a bank vault. Be good chaps now and come out holding your hands in the air."

It did not occur to Agent Jones that it is rather difficult to crawl on your hands and knees while at the same time holding your hands in the air. Nevertheless, the four men, including those who had called themselves Ross Duncan and Clayton Jones emerged from the vault and were immediately handcuffed by Agent Jones and his band of constables.

"The paddy wagon is on its way, sir," said one of the young constables.

"Excellent," said Agent Jones. "Mr. Holmes, yet again you have proved your mettle. Your ways are passing strange but they have worked and we have got the rascals without having to fire a shot. Indeed, they have caught themselves." He chuckled at his own wit.

"Officer Jones," said the Colonel as we made our way up the stairs, "It may be that I have lost my ability to count. But I rather distinctly recall that there was a total of five rascals, and all I see now is four. I do believe that we still have a job to do to find number five."

"Quite right, sir. My men will scour the neighborhood and I am sure that the final villain shall be arrested forthwith."

"I thought my wife would have come out to join us," said Jabez Darby. "Let me fetch her and we can all go for a morning cup of tea to celebrate. He walked towards the back of the store and entered the office portion, the center of all of our operations. A moment later he came back out, but was alone.

"She is not here. Did she already come out? Did you or your men see her, Agent Jones?"

"No sir. I did not see her. Let me ask my men." He left us for a minute and returned looking perplexed, bordering on worry. "No sir. None of my men have seen her."

I could see a strange look coming over the face of Sherlock Holmes. It was the same look I had seen several weeks ago in Baker Street when he learned that Professor Moriarty was behind the grand scheme of fraud. "Agent Jones," he said. "Could you please summon every available constable at once and have them begin a thorough search of the neighborhood? Mrs. Darby may be in very grave danger."

The police agent was about to blow on his whistle to bring his men together when a boy ran up to us. "Is one of you Sherlock Holmes?" he asked. Holmes confirmed that it was he, and the lad gave him a note that Holmes read in the early light. The look of fear on his face deepened and I saw his lower lip begin to quiver ever so slightly.

"Dear God, Watson, he has her."

He read us the note:

```
Release the men immediately. Give them
safe passage back to the station and
allow them to board the London train.

If you do not heed these instructions,
your next search will be for Mrs.
Darby's dead and violated body. You
have fifteen minutes to comply.
```

"We have to release them, we have to!" cried out Jabez Darby. "You must let them go, Officer, you have to. She will be murdered!"

The young man was in a dreadful state of panic. He grabbed at the arm of the officer and pleaded with him.

"Jabez," said Holmes, "please believe me. If we release them he will only laugh at us, kidnap your wife and at some later time subject her to the most degrading and painful death. He is a monster. He is inhuman. And now that we have destroyed his diabolical scheme he will wreak revenge for no other reason than to assuage his anger."

"What can we do then?" shouted the young husband in distress.

"We must rely on the constables to cut off all of the roads and alleys, and guard the station. They will begin to do that straightaway. They will search all the buildings and hiding places within several blocks. He cannot have taken her far."

"That's not enough! He said he will kill her!" In a very quick motion, Jabez Darby grabbed one of the Colonel's revolvers out of its holster and turned and ran out of the office and into the street.

"Sir! Stop!" shouted the Police Agent. "You cannot run out alone. It is not safe." Agent Jones immediately ran after him. A few seconds later we heard the crack of a rifle shot from the street. Holmes and I looked at each other in panic and ran towards the door. The Colonel was already in front of us with a revolver in his hand. We entered the street and saw that Agent Jones was holding the ankles of Jabez Darby, having tackled him on the run. Neither appeared to be wounded.

I heard a scream, a man's voice, from across the road and looked up through the fog in time to see a flailing body fall from the third-floor balcony of the building and land in the street. The man landed feet first and must have injured himself badly as he struggled to get to his feet. He steadied himself and began to raise a rifle towards us. Agent Jones went after him like a tiger. In the short moment before he could take aim Jones was upon him, pushed the rifle away with his left hand and with the nightstick in his right hand laid a crack on the man's head that could be heard a block away. He crumbled into a sorry heap on the roadway. Three young constables were on him and handcuffed and removed his rifle and other arms.

Jabez Darby was standing in the middle of the street still in fear and terror. In the faint light and early morning fog, his gaze was moving wildly back and forth over the building from which the would-be killer had fallen.

From within the street level doorway, we heard a woman's voice call out. "Jabez, darling! It's alright. I am here. I am safe." Mrs. Miriam Darby came running out to the street and threw herself into her husband's arms. They held each other, trembling.

More constables and the paddy wagon had appeared out of the early morning light and fog. The four men were marched from the bank vault and into it. The injured rifleman was lifted up and laid on the floor.

"Holmes," I said *sotto voce.* "Look. Down the road."

In the gloomy light, we observed the figure of a tall, thin man, dressed in a black ulster and wearing a top hat. We could see that he was looking at us. Slowly he raised his walking stick high in the air above his head and then lowered it until it was pointing directly at us, as if he were a sorcerer casting an evil spell. He held that position for several seconds, and then turned to his right and vanished into an alleyway.

"Professor Moriarty is not a happy man," mused Sherlock Holmes. "However, it is unlikely that he will bother this family again. It is I who has become the object of his hatred."

With an air of affected nonchalance, Holmes looked at the group of us and said, "Might I treat my Company of Irregulars to a cup of morning tea? I do believe that we have all earned one."

We pasted on our brave faces and made our way back to The Duke. After some forced idle chit-chat, Agent Jones nodded respectfully towards Mrs. Darby and said, "Madam Darby, I know that what happened was very trying and although it should not be necessary to have a sworn statement given at the police station, I must ask you to tell me what happened to you and the nature of your fortunate escape."

Miriam Darby took a slow sip of her tea, drew a deep breath and began her story.

"As soon as all of the noise and commotion began in the basement, I, unwisely it now seems, but not wanting to miss out on what was happening, came out of the back office and into the store. I was met there by an unknown man who immediately grabbed my arm and placed a revolver under my chin. He commanded me to be silent and come with him, and I had no doubt he would kill me if I refused. I did as he ordered, commending my soul to my Maker and giving a desperate prayer for my husband and children who I feared might never see me again.

"He led me into the building across the way. As it was still before daybreak and a Saturday morning, it was empty. He forced me up two flights of stairs and into a room that looked out over the street. He stood by the window and every so often looked back at me and waved his revolver in my direction. We could hear the goings on from the bookstore and I heard my husband cry out and the Police Agent's shout to him.

"At that instant, the villain put down his revolver and quickly removed his rifle from his back. I heard him say, 'Lovely, a bright bald head gleaming through the fog. A perfect target.'

"I was petrified by fear, but the Lord intervened and I found the strength to rush towards him."

Here she stopped and took another slow sip of tea.

"Yes madam," said Peter Jones. "Pray continue."

She looked at him and quietly said, "Sir, as you can see, I am not a small woman, and the villain who was shooting at my husband was not a very large man."

For a moment, no one spoke as it became clear to us that this devout Christian lady had tossed an armed man off of a balcony and into the street. I sensed that this act, although frightfully brave, was not one that she wished to be attached to her reputation for the rest of her life.

Holmes had reached the same conclusion and turned to Agent Jones. "It is a common characteristic of the criminal class, is it not sir, that they try to brace themselves with copious amounts of alcohol before engaging in a dastardly crime?"

The agent looked at Holmes curiously for a moment and then broke into a smile. "Right you are, Mr. Holmes. I swear that nasty blackguard stunk to high heaven of gin. Drunken sot he was. Couldn't even fire a shot from a balcony without toppling off. That's the way it is with drink. It will bring you down every time, if you know what I mean. It will bring you down." He laughed loudly at his witticism.

Epilogue

The rest of the fall of 1890 passed peacefully. The winter was one of the coldest on record. I began to publish stories about Sherlock Holmes in *The Strand,* a practice I would continue for many years thereafter. The first station of the Underground was opened by the Prince of Wales. So many men, women, and children were fleeing the hard life of Europe for America that the Americans opened a special receiving center on Ellis Island. It was destined to become the gateway to a new life, the American dream, for millions who would follow. February of the following year brought England one of its worst blizzards ever and it was weeks before the snow finally melted and the warmth of spring returned.

On a lovely Sunday in April, I received a note from Sherlock Holmes asking if I would join him in the early afternoon as he was expecting visitors and thought I might wish to greet them as well. I came with no idea who he was expecting and sat down beside Holmes in the comfortable and familiar room at 221B Baker Street. Mrs. Hudson had prepared us a delicious lunch, after which we sat in our traditional chairs and Holmes lit up his pipe.

It was at that moment that Mrs. Hudson entered and said, "There is a family down on the sidewalk, sir. I asked them to come up, but they declined and asked only that you might take a moment to say hello as they passed."

Holmes rose, pipe in hand, and descended that stairs. I followed close behind.

On Baker Street, we were greeted by an attractive and stylishly dressed young family. A mother, father and two adorable children smiled and addressed us by name. The young husband tipped his hat towards us, displaying as thick a head of chestnut hair as I have ever seen.

"Goodness gracious, Jabez Darby!" I blurted out joyfully. "You look wonderful. All of you. Magnificent." Mrs. Miriam Darby introduced us to her beautiful children who politely extended their hands to both Sherlock Holmes and me.

"This is a delight," I said. "What has brought you and your lovely family to London?"

"We moved here last week, Doctor Watson," Jabez replied. "We attended services this morning at the Gospel Hall by Marylebone and knew that we just had to call upon you on our way back to our new home.

"At the time we met you, Mr. Holmes," he continued, "we could not have known that you would be like an angel of light in our lives. You were truly an answer to our prayers and the instrument used by the Lord to deliver us from evil. We thank God every night for you."

This was a bit too much for me and I made as if I were looking at Holmes's back and above his head for the wings and halo. Holmes gave me a bit of a look and I confess that I struggled to conceal a smirk.

Holmes responded to his visitors graciously. "And what of your bookstore. How is The Little Flock managing without its shepherds?"

"I gave the management of it over to one of our elders who had recently retired, and had a decent pension from the government on which to live. He is as happy as a clam sitting and reading and chatting with the occasional customer, and his wife has thanked me a hundred times over for getting him out of the house.

"And this, thanks to you and the mysterious ways of the Lord, is what I am now doing."

He handed his card to Holmes, who smiled and gave it to me.

The Brain Fever Trust

Jabez Nelson Darby
General Secretary

Bedford Row, London

"It gave me such satisfaction when I was working every day for a good cause that did not even exist, that I went ahead and set up the Trust on my own. Then I sent out all those letters and applications I had prepared, and many of them were returned with generous donations. With the help of a learned group of doctors we are providing the money needed for medical research, and at the same time giving help and encouragement to those who are suffering.

"My medical advisors have suggested that we change the name since they are starting to call the malady from which I suffered *clinical depression,* but that can wait until we are better established. I am enjoying my life and career as never before, gentlemen, and I cannot thank you often enough."

"The smiles on your face and those of you wife and children," said Holmes with authentic grace, "are all the thanks we shall ever need." He gave the young gentleman a pat on the shoulder, all the while continuing to puff on his beloved pipe.

"And you my good lady," he said with a twinkle in his eye as he warmly regarded Mrs. Miriam Darby. "What might you be up to when you are no longer escorting drunken villains off of balconies?"

She gave a peal of delighted laughter and handed us her card.

Miriam Darby (Mrs.)

Private Investment Consultant

Bond Court, City of London

"After our adventure, the Colonel and I became great friends and formed a business partnership. It turned out that he is a devoted Southern Baptist gentleman, and their beliefs are not that much distant from ours as to have me unequally yoked. So he quit Western Union and we went into business together. He has become an honorary grandfather to my children."

"And your new business, if I may ask?" said Holmes.

"The Lord is blessing us beyond all we could ask or imagine," she replied. "We have rather quickly acquired a reputation for expertise concerning firms that are traded both in New York and in The City and are quite sought after."

"Some three thousand years ago," said Jabez Darby, "my namesake in the Bible – you will find his story in the First Book of Chronicles – prayed to the God of Israel, "Oh that thou wouldest bless me indeed and enlarge my coast, and that thine hand might be with me, and that thou wouldest keep me from evil." That prayer has been answered many times over in my life. We are blessed with friends and family and with fearless protectors, sir."

Miriam Darby looked up at Holmes and asked, "And you sir? And you, our wonderful Doctor? We trust and pray that you are well."

Holmes took a slow draw on his pipe and exhaled it even more slowly. "Other than continuing to defile my 'temple of the Holy Spirit' as you called it, we could not be happier. You would agree, Doctor Watson?"

"Most assuredly."

"In that case," said Mrs. Darby, "all you have to do is stop putting that dreadful poison into your body." With this she quickly snatched the pipe right out of Holmes's mouth, gave the bowl of it a smart rap on the heel of her boot, and handed it back, empty and extinguished, to the nonplused Holmes and said, "Then you will be a healthier man and, as a result, a better detective, Mr. Sherlock Holmes."

With a beaming smile, she threw her arms around Holmes's neck and planted a kiss firmly on his cheek.

Dear reader:

Did you enjoy this story? Are there ways it could have been improved? Please help the author and future readers of New Sherlock Holmes Mysteries by leaving a constructive review on the site from which you acquired it and on Goodreads. Thank you,   CSC

About the Author

Once upon a time Craig Stephen Copland was an English major and studied under both Northrop Frye and Marshall McLuhan at the University of Toronto way back in the 1960s. He never got over his spiritual attraction to great literature and captivating stories. Somewhere in the decades since he became a dedicated Sherlockian. He is a member of the Sherlock Holmes Society of Canada, (www.torontobootmakers.com), and, like his Sherlockian colleagues, addicted to the sacred canon. In May of 2014 the Bootmakers announced a contest for a new Sherlock Holmes mystery. Although he had no previous experience writing fiction he entered and was blessed to be declared one of the winners. So he kept writing more stories and is now on a mission to write sixty new Sherlock Holmes mysteries – each one inspired by one of the original stories in The

He has been writing these stories while living in Toronto, New York, Tokyo, Buenos Aires, Bahrain and the Okanagan Valley. If you have a suggestion for a new Sherlock Holmes mystery, please contact him at craigstephencopland@gmail.com.

New Sherlock Holmes Mysteries

by Craig Stephen Copland

www.SherlockHolmesMystery.com

This is the first book in the series. Start with it and enjoy MORE SHERLOCK.

Studying Scarlet. Starlet O'Halloran, a fabulous mature woman, who reminds the reader of Scarlet O'Hara (but who, for copyright reasons cannot actually be her) has arrived in London looking for her long-lost husband, Brett (who resembles Rhett Butler, but who, for copyright reasons, cannot actually be him). She enlists the help of Sherlock Holmes. This is an unauthorized parody, inspired by Arthur Conan Doyle's *A Study in Scarlet* and Margaret Mitchell's *Gone with the Wind.*

Six new Sherlock Holmes stories are always free to enjoy. If you have not already read them, go to this site, sign up, download and enjoy. www.SherlockHolmesMystery.com

Super Collections A, B and C

57 New Sherlock Holmes Mysteries.

The perfect ebooks for readers who subscribe to Kindle Unlimited

Enter 'Craig Stephen Copland Sherlock Holmes Super Collection' into your Amazon search bar. Enjoy over 2 million words of MORE SHERLOCK.

www.SherlockHolmesMystery.com

The Red-Headed League

The Original
Sherlock Holmes Story

SIR ARTHUR CONAN DOYLE

The Red-Headed League

I had called upon my friend, Mr. Sherlock Holmes, one day in the autumn of last year and found him in deep conversation with a very stout, florid-faced, elderly gentleman with fiery red hair. With an apology for my intrusion, I was about to withdraw when Holmes pulled me abruptly into the room and closed the door behind me.

"You could not possibly have come at a better time, my dear Watson," he said cordially.

"I was afraid that you were engaged."

"So I am. Very much so."

"Then I can wait in the next room."

"Not at all. This gentleman, Mr. Wilson, has been my partner and helper in many of my most successful cases, and I have no doubt that he will be of the utmost use to me in yours also."

The stout gentleman half rose from his chair and gave a bob of greeting, with a quick little questioning glance from his small fat-encircled eyes.

"Try the settee," said Holmes, relapsing into his armchair and putting his fingertips together, as was his custom when in judicial moods. "I know, my dear Watson, that you share my love of all that is bizarre and outside the conventions and humdrum routine of everyday life. You have shown your relish for it by the enthusiasm which has prompted you to chronicle, and, if you will excuse my saying so, somewhat to embellish so many of my own little adventures."

"Your cases have indeed been of the greatest interest to me," I observed.

"You will remember that I remarked the other day, just before we went into the very simple problem presented by Miss Mary Sutherland, that for strange effects and extraordinary combinations we must go to life itself, which is always far more daring than any effort of the imagination."

"A proposition which I took the liberty of doubting."

"You did, Doctor, but none the less you must come round to my view, for otherwise I shall keep on piling fact upon fact on you until your reason breaks down under them and acknowledges me to be right. Now, Mr. Jabez Wilson here has been good enough to call upon me this morning, and to begin a narrative which promises to be one of the most singular which I have listened to for some time. You have heard me remark that the strangest and most unique things are very often connected not with the larger but with the smaller crimes, and occasionally, indeed, where there is room for doubt whether any positive crime has been committed. As far as I have heard, it is impossible for me to say whether the present case is an instance of crime or not, but the course of events is certainly among the most singular that I have ever listened to. Perhaps, Mr. Wilson, you would have the great kindness to recommence your narrative. I ask you not merely because my friend Dr. Watson has not heard the opening part but also because the peculiar nature of the story makes me anxious to have every possible detail from your lips. As a rule, when I have heard some slight indication of the course of events, I am able to guide myself by the thousands of other similar cases which occur to my memory. In the present instance I am forced to admit that the facts are, to the best of my belief, unique."

The portly client puffed out his chest with an appearance of some little pride and pulled a dirty and wrinkled newspaper from the inside pocket of his greatcoat. As he glanced down the advertisement column, with his head thrust forward and the paper flattened out upon his knee, I took a good look at the man and endeavored, after the fashion of my companion, to read the indications which might be presented by his dress or appearance.

I did not gain very much, however, by my inspection. Our visitor bore every mark of being an average commonplace British tradesman, obese, pompous, and slow. He wore rather baggy grey shepherd's check trousers, a not over-clean black frock-coat, unbuttoned in the front, and a drab waistcoat with a heavy brassy Albert chain, and a square pierced bit of metal dangling down as an ornament. A frayed top-hat and a faded brown overcoat with a wrinkled velvet collar lay upon a chair beside him. Altogether, look as I would, there was nothing remarkable about the man save his blazing red head, and the expression of extreme chagrin and discontent upon his features.

Sherlock Holmes' quick eye took in my occupation, and he shook his head with a smile as he noticed my questioning glances. "Beyond the obvious facts that he has at some time done manual Labour, that he takes snuff, that he is a Freemason, that he has been in China, and that he has done a considerable amount of writing lately, I can deduce nothing else."

Mr. Jabez Wilson started up in his chair, with his forefinger upon the paper, but his eyes upon my companion.

"How, in the name of good-fortune, did you know all that, Mr. Holmes?" he asked. "How did you know, for example, that I did manual Labour. It's as true as gospel, for I began as a ship's carpenter."

"Your hands, my dear sir. Your right hand is quite a size larger than your left. You have worked with it, and the muscles are more developed."

"Well, the snuff, then, and the Freemasonry?"

"I won't insult your intelligence by telling you how I read that, especially as, rather against the strict rules of your order, you use an arc-and-compass breastpin."

"Ah, of course, I forgot that. But the writing?"

"What else can be indicated by that right cuff so very shiny for five inches, and the left one with the smooth patch near the elbow where you rest it upon the desk?"

"Well, but China?"

"The fish that you have tattooed immediately above your right wrist could only have been done in China. I have made a small study of tattoo marks and have even contributed to the literature of the subject. That trick of staining the fishes' scales of a delicate pink is quite peculiar to China. When, in addition, I see a Chinese coin hanging from your watch-chain, the matter becomes even more simple."

Mr. Jabez Wilson laughed heavily. "Well, I never!" said he. "I thought at first that you had done something clever, but I see that there was nothing in it after all."

"I begin to think, Watson," said Holmes, "that I make a mistake in explaining. '*Omne ignotum pro magnifico*,' you know, and my poor little reputation, such as it is, will suffer shipwreck if I am so candid. Can you not find the advertisement, Mr. Wilson?"

"Yes, I have got it now," he answered with his thick red finger planted halfway down the column. "Here it is. This is what began it all. You just read it for yourself, sir."

I took the paper from him and read as follows:

"TO THE RED-HEADED LEAGUE: On account of the bequest of the late Ezekiah Hopkins, of Lebanon, Pennsylvania, U. S. A., there is now another vacancy open which entitles a member of the League to a salary of £4 a week for purely nominal services. All red-headed men who are sound in body and mind and above the age of twenty-one years, are eligible. Apply in person on Monday, at eleven o'clock, to Duncan Ross, at the offices of the League, 7 Pope's Court, Fleet Street."

"What on earth does this mean?" I ejaculated after I had twice read over the extraordinary announcement.

Holmes chuckled and wriggled in his chair, as was his habit when in high spirits. "It is a little off the beaten track, isn't it?" said he. "And now, Mr. Wilson, off you go at scratch and tell us all about yourself, your household, and the effect which this advertisement had upon your fortunes. You will first make a note, Doctor, of the paper and the date."

"It is *The Morning Chronicle* of April 27, 1890. Just two months ago."

"Very good. Now, Mr. Wilson?"

"Well, it is just as I have been telling you, Mr. Sherlock Holmes," said Jabez Wilson, mopping his forehead; "I have a small pawnbroker's business at Coburg Square, near the City. It's not a very large affair, and of late years it has not done more than just give me a living. I used to be able to keep two assistants, but now I only keep one; and I would have a job to pay him but that he is willing to come for half wages so as to learn the business."

"What is the name of this obliging youth?" asked Sherlock Holmes.

"His name is Vincent Spaulding, and he's not such a youth, either. It's hard to say his age. I should not wish a smarter assistant, Mr. Holmes; and I know very well that he could better himself and earn twice what I am able to give him. But, after all, if he is satisfied, why should I put ideas in his head?"

"Why, indeed? You seem most fortunate in having an employee who comes under the full market price. It is not a common experience among employers in this age. I don't know that your assistant is not as remarkable as your advertisement."

"Oh, he has his faults, too," said Mr. Wilson. "Never was such a fellow for photography. Snapping away with a camera when he ought to be improving his mind, and then diving down into the cellar like a rabbit into its hole to develop his pictures. That is his main fault, but on the whole he's a good worker. There's no vice in him."

"He is still with you, I presume?"

"Yes, sir. He and a girl of fourteen, who does a bit of simple cooking and keeps the place clean—that's all I have in the house, for I am a widower and never had any family. We live very quietly, sir, the three of us; and we keep a roof over our heads and pay our debts, if we do nothing more.

"The first thing that put us out was that advertisement. Spaulding, he came down into the office just this day eight weeks, with this very paper in his hand, and he says:

" 'I wish to the Lord, Mr. Wilson, that I was a red-headed man.'

" 'Why that?' I asks.

" 'Why,' says he, 'here's another vacancy on the League of the Red-headed Men. It's worth quite a little fortune to any man who gets it, and I understand that there are more vacancies than there are men, so that the trustees are at their wits' end what to do with the money. If my hair would only change color, here's a nice little crib all ready for me to step into.'

" 'Why, what is it, then?' I asked. You see, Mr. Holmes, I am a very stay-at-home man, and as my business came to me instead of my having to go to it, I was often weeks on end without putting my foot over the door-mat. In that way I didn't know much of what was going on outside, and I was always glad of a bit of news.

" 'Have you never heard of the League of the Red-headed Men?' he asked with his eyes open.

" 'Never.'

" 'Why, I wonder at that, for you are eligible yourself for one of the vacancies.'

" 'And what are they worth?' I asked.

" 'Oh, merely a couple of hundred a year, but the work is slight, and it need not interfere very much with one's other occupations.'

"Well, you can easily think that that made me prick up my ears, for the business has not been over good for some years, and an extra couple of hundred would have been very handy.

" 'Tell me all about it,' said I.

" 'Well,' said he, showing me the advertisement, 'you can see for yourself that the League has a vacancy, and there is the address where you should apply for particulars. As far as I can make out, the League was founded by an American millionaire, Ezekiah Hopkins, who was very peculiar in his ways. He was himself red-headed, and he had a great sympathy for all red-headed men; so, when he died, it was found that he had left his enormous fortune in the hands of trustees, with instructions to apply the interest to the providing of easy berths to men whose hair is of that color. From all I hear it is splendid pay and very little to do.'

" 'But,' said I, 'there would be millions of red-headed men who would apply.'

" 'Not so many as you might think,' he answered. 'You see it is really confined to Londoners, and to grown men. This American had started from London when he was young, and he wanted to do the old town a good turn. Then, again, I have heard it is no use your applying if your hair is light red, or dark red, or anything but real bright, blazing, fiery red. Now, if you cared to apply, Mr. Wilson, you would just walk in; but perhaps it would hardly be worth your while to put yourself out of the way for the sake of a few hundred pounds.'

"Now, it is a fact, gentlemen, as you may see for yourselves, that my hair is of a very full and rich tint, so that it seemed to me that if there was to be any competition in the matter I stood as good a chance as any man that I had ever met. Vincent Spaulding seemed to know so much about it that I thought he might prove useful, so I just ordered him to put up the shutters for the day and to come right away with me. He was very willing to have a holiday, so we shut the business up and started off for the address that was given us in the advertisement.

"I never hope to see such a sight as that again, Mr. Holmes. From north, south, east, and west every man who had a shade of red in his hair had tramped into the city to answer the advertisement. Fleet Street was choked with red-headed folk, and Pope's Court looked like a coster's orange barrow. I should not have thought there were so many in the whole country as were brought together by that single advertisement. Every shade of color they were—straw, lemon, orange, brick, Irish-setter, liver, clay; but, as Spaulding said, there were not many who had the real vivid flame-colored tint. When I saw how many were waiting, I would have given it up in despair; but Spaulding would not hear of it. How he did it I could not imagine, but he pushed and pulled and butted until he got me through the crowd, and right up to the steps which led to the office. There was a double stream upon the stair, some going up in hope, and some coming back dejected; but we wedged in as well as we could and soon found ourselves in the office."

"Your experience has been a most entertaining one," remarked Holmes as his client paused and refreshed his memory with a huge pinch of snuff. "Pray continue your very interesting statement."

"There was nothing in the office but a couple of wooden chairs and a deal table, behind which sat a small man with a head that was even redder than mine. He said a few words to each candidate as he came up, and then he always managed to find some fault in them which would disqualify them. Getting a vacancy did not seem to be such a very easy matter, after all. However, when our turn came the little man was much more favorable to me than to any of the others, and he closed the door as we entered, so that he might have a private word with us.

" 'This is Mr. Jabez Wilson,' said my assistant, 'and he is willing to fill a vacancy in the League.'

" 'And he is admirably suited for it,' the other answered. 'He has every requirement. I cannot recall when I have seen anything so fine.' He took a step backward, cocked his head on one side, and gazed at my hair until I felt quite bashful. Then suddenly he plunged forward, wrung my hand, and congratulated me warmly on my success.

" 'It would be injustice to hesitate,' said he. 'You will, however, I am sure, excuse me for taking an obvious precaution.' With that he seized my hair in both his hands, and tugged until I yelled with the pain. 'There is water in your eyes,' said he as he released me. 'I perceive that all is as it should be. But we have to be careful, for we have twice been deceived by wigs and once by paint. I could tell you tales of cobbler's wax which would disgust you with human nature.' He stepped over to the window and shouted through it at the top of his voice that the vacancy was filled. A groan of disappointment came up from below, and the folk all trooped away in different directions until there was not a red-head to be seen except my own and that of the manager.

" 'My name,' said he, 'is Mr. Duncan Ross, and I am myself one of the pensioners upon the fund left by our noble benefactor. Are you a married man, Mr. Wilson? Have you a family?'

"I answered that I had not.

"His face fell immediately.

" 'Dear me!' he said gravely, 'that is very serious indeed! I am sorry to hear you say that. The fund was, of course, for the propagation and spread of the red-heads as well as for their maintenance. It is exceedingly unfortunate that you should be a bachelor.'

"My face lengthened at this, Mr. Holmes, for I thought that I was not to have the vacancy after all; but after thinking it over for a few minutes he said that it would be all right.

" 'In the case of another,' said he, 'the objection might be fatal, but we must stretch a point in favour of a man with such a head of hair as yours. When shall you be able to enter upon your new duties?'

" 'Well, it is a little awkward, for I have a business already,' said I.

" 'Oh, never mind about that, Mr. Wilson!' said Vincent Spaulding. 'I should be able to look after that for you.'

" 'What would be the hours?' I asked.

" 'Ten to two.'

"Now a pawnbroker's business is mostly done of an evening, Mr. Holmes, especially Thursday and Friday evening, which is just before pay-day; so it would suit me very well to earn a little in the mornings. Besides, I knew that my assistant was a good man, and that he would see to anything that turned up.

" 'That would suit me very well,' said I. 'And the pay?'

" 'Is £4 a week.'

" 'And the work?'

" 'Is purely nominal.'

" 'What do you call purely nominal?'

" 'Well, you have to be in the office, or at least in the building, the whole time. If you leave, you forfeit your whole position forever. The will is very clear upon that point. You don't comply with the conditions if you budge from the office during that time.'

" 'It's only four hours a day, and I should not think of leaving,' said I.

" 'No excuse will avail,' said Mr. Duncan Ross; 'neither sickness nor business nor anything else. There you must stay, or you lose your billet.'

" 'And the work?'

" 'Is to copy out the *Encyclopedia Britannica*. There is the first volume of it in that press. You must find your own ink, pens, and blotting-paper, but we provide this table and chair. Will you be ready to-morrow?'

" 'Certainly,' I answered.

" 'Then, good-bye, Mr. Jabez Wilson, and let me congratulate you once more on the important position which you have been fortunate enough to gain.' He bowed me out of the room and I went home with my assistant, hardly knowing what to say or do, I was so pleased at my own good fortune.

"Well, I thought over the matter all day, and by evening I was in low spirits again; for I had quite persuaded myself that the whole affair must be some great hoax or fraud, though what its object might be I could not imagine. It seemed altogether past belief that anyone could make such a will, or that they would pay such a sum for doing anything so simple as copying out the *Encyclopedia Britannica*. Vincent

Spaulding did what he could to cheer me up, but by bedtime I had reasoned myself out of the whole thing. However, in the morning I determined to have a look at it anyhow, so I bought a penny bottle of ink, and with a quill-pen, and seven sheets of foolscap paper, I started off for Pope's Court.

"Well, to my surprise and delight, everything was as right as possible. The table was set out ready for me, and Mr. Duncan Ross was there to see that I got fairly to work. He started me off upon the letter A, and then he left me; but he would drop in from time to time to see that all was right with me. At two o'clock he bade me good-day, complimented me upon the amount that I had written, and locked the door of the office after me.

"This went on day after day, Mr. Holmes, and on Saturday the manager came in and planked down four golden sovereigns for my week's work. It was the same next week, and the same the week after. Every morning I was there at ten, and every afternoon I left at two. By degrees Mr. Duncan Ross took to coming in only once of a morning, and then, after a time, he did not come in at all. Still, of course, I never dared to leave the room for an instant, for I was not sure when he might come, and the billet was such a good one, and suited me so well, that I would not risk the loss of it.

"Eight weeks passed away like this, and I had written about Abbots and Archery and Armor and Architecture and Attica, and hoped with diligence that I might get on to the B's before very long. It cost me something in foolscap, and I had pretty nearly filled a shelf with my writings. And then suddenly the whole business came to an end."

"To an end?"

"Yes, sir. And no later than this morning. I went to my work as usual at ten o'clock, but the door was shut and locked, with a little square of cardboard hammered on to the middle of the panel with a tack. Here it is, and you can read for yourself."

He held up a piece of white cardboard about the size of a sheet of note-paper. It read in this fashion:

THE RED-HEADED LEAGUE
IS
DISSOLVED.

October 9, 1890.

Sherlock Holmes and I surveyed this curt announcement and the rueful face behind it, until the comical side of the affair so completely overtopped every other consideration that we both burst out into a roar of laughter.

"I cannot see that there is anything very funny," cried our client, flushing up to the roots of his flaming head. "If you can do nothing better than laugh at me, I can go elsewhere."

"No, no," cried Holmes, shoving him back into the chair from which he had half risen. "I really wouldn't miss your case for the world. It is most refreshingly unusual. But there is, if you will excuse my saying so, something just a little funny about it. Pray what steps did you take when you found the card upon the door?"

"I was staggered, sir. I did not know what to do. Then I called at the offices round, but none of them seemed to know anything about it. Finally, I went to the landlord, who is an accountant living on the ground floor, and I asked him if he could tell me what had become of the Red-headed League. He said that he had never heard of any such body. Then I asked him who Mr. Duncan Ross was. He answered that the name was new to him.

" 'Well,' said I, 'the gentleman at No. 4.'

" 'What, the red-headed man?'

" 'Yes.'

" 'Oh,' said he, 'his name was William Morris. He was a solicitor and was using my room as a temporary convenience until his new premises were ready. He moved out yesterday.'

" 'Where could I find him?'

" 'Oh, at his new offices. He did tell me the address. Yes, 17 King Edward Street, near St. Paul's.'

"I started off, Mr. Holmes, but when I got to that address it was a manufactory of artificial knee-caps, and no one in it had ever heard of either Mr. William Morris or Mr. Duncan Ross."

"And what did you do then?" asked Holmes.

"I went home to Saxe-Coburg Square, and I took the advice of my assistant. But he could not help me in any way. He could only say that if I waited I should hear by post. But that was not quite good enough, Mr. Holmes. I did not wish to lose such a place without a struggle, so, as I had heard that you were good enough to give advice to poor folk who were in need of it, I came right away to you."

"And you did very wisely," said Holmes. "Your case is an exceedingly remarkable one, and I shall be happy to look into it. From what you have told me I think that it is possible that graver issues hang from it than might at first sight appear."

"Grave enough!" said Mr. Jabez Wilson. "Why, I have lost four pound a week."

"As far as you are personally concerned," remarked Holmes, "I do not see that you have any grievance against this extraordinary league. On the contrary, you are, as I understand, richer by some £30, to say nothing of the minute knowledge which you have gained on every subject which comes under the letter A. You have lost nothing by them."

"No, sir. But I want to find out about them, and who they are, and what their object was in playing this prank—if it was a prank—

upon me. It was a pretty expensive joke for them, for it cost them two and thirty pounds."

"We shall endeavor to clear up these points for you. And, first, one or two questions, Mr. Wilson. This assistant of yours who first called your attention to the advertisement—how long had he been with you?"

"About a month then."

"How did he come?"

"In answer to an advertisement."

"Was he the only applicant?"

"No, I had a dozen."

"Why did you pick him?"

"Because he was handy and would come cheap."

"At half wages, in fact."

"Yes."

"What is he like, this Vincent Spaulding?"

"Small, stout-built, very quick in his ways, no hair on his face, though he's not short of thirty. Has a white splash of acid upon his forehead."

Holmes sat up in his chair in considerable excitement. "I thought as much," said he. "Have you ever observed that his ears are pierced for earrings?"

"Yes, sir. He told me that a gipsy had done it for him when he was a lad."

"Hum!" said Holmes, sinking back in deep thought. "He is still with you?"

"Oh, yes, sir; I have only just left him."

"And has your business been attended to in your absence?"

"Nothing to complain of, sir. There's never very much to do of a morning."

"That will do, Mr. Wilson. I shall be happy to give you an opinion upon the subject in the course of a day or two. To-day is Saturday, and I hope that by Monday we may come to a conclusion."

"Well, Watson," said Holmes when our visitor had left us, "what do you make of it all?"

"I make nothing of it," I answered frankly. "It is a most mysterious business."

"As a rule," said Holmes, "the more bizarre a thing is the less mysterious it proves to be. It is your commonplace, featureless crimes which are really puzzling, just as a commonplace face is the most difficult to identify. But I must be prompt over this matter."

"What are you going to do, then?" I asked.

"To smoke," he answered. "It is quite a three pipe problem, and I beg that you won't speak to me for fifty minutes." He curled himself up in his chair, with his thin knees drawn up to his hawk-like nose, and there he sat with his eyes closed and his black clay pipe thrusting out like the bill of some strange bird. I had come to the conclusion that he had dropped asleep, and indeed was nodding myself, when he suddenly sprang out of his chair with the gesture of a man who has made up his mind and put his pipe down upon the mantelpiece.

"Sarasate plays at the St. James's Hall this afternoon," he remarked. "What do you think, Watson? Could your patients spare you for a few hours?"

"I have nothing to do to-day. My practice is never very absorbing."

"Then put on your hat and come. I am going through the City first, and we can have some lunch on the way. I observe that there is a good deal of German music on the programmed, which is rather more

106

to my taste than Italian or French. It is introspective, and I want to introspect. Come along!"

We travelled by the Underground as far as Aldersgate; and a short walk took us to Saxe-Coburg Square, the scene of the singular story which we had listened to in the morning. It was a poky, little, shabby-genteel place, where four lines of dingy two-storied brick houses looked out into a small railed-in enclosure, where a lawn of weedy grass and a few clumps of faded laurel bushes made a hard fight against a smoke-laden and uncongenial atmosphere. Three gilt balls and a brown board with "JABEZ WILSON" in white letters, upon a corner house, announced the place where our red-headed client carried on his business. Sherlock Holmes stopped in front of it with his head on one side and looked it all over, with his eyes shining brightly between puckered lids. Then he walked slowly up the street, and then down again to the corner, still looking keenly at the houses. Finally he returned to the pawnbroker's, and, having thumped vigorously upon the pavement with his stick two or three times, he went up to the door and knocked. It was instantly opened by a bright-looking, clean-shaven young fellow, who asked him to step in.

"Thank you," said Holmes, "I only wished to ask you how you would go from here to the Strand."

"Third right, fourth left," answered the assistant promptly, closing the door.

"Smart fellow, that," observed Holmes as we walked away. "He is, in my judgment, the fourth smartest man in London, and for daring I am not sure that he has not a claim to be third. I have known something of him before."

"Evidently," said I, "Mr. Wilson's assistant counts for a good deal in this mystery of the Red-headed League. I am sure that you inquired your way merely in order that you might see him."

"Not him."

"What then?"

"The knees of his trousers."

"And what did you see?"

"What I expected to see."

"Why did you beat the pavement?"

"My dear doctor, this is a time for observation, not for talk. We are spies in an enemy's country. We know something of Saxe-Coburg Square. Let us now explore the parts which lie behind it."

The road in which we found ourselves as we turned round the corner from the retired Saxe-Coburg Square presented as great a contrast to it as the front of a picture does to the back. It was one of the main arteries which conveyed the traffic of the City to the north and west. The roadway was blocked with the immense stream of commerce flowing in a double tide inward and outward, while the footpaths were black with the hurrying swarm of pedestrians. It was difficult to realize as we looked at the line of fine shops and stately business premises that they really abutted on the other side upon the faded and stagnant square which we had just quitted.

"Let me see," said Holmes, standing at the corner and glancing along the line, "I should like just to remember the order of the houses here. It is a hobby of mine to have an exact knowledge of London. There is Mortimer's, the tobacconist, the little newspaper shop, the Coburg branch of the City and Suburban Bank, the Vegetarian Restaurant, and McFarlane's carriage-building depot. That carries us right on to the other block. And now, Doctor, we've done our work, so it's time we had some play. A sandwich and a cup of coffee, and then off to violin-land, where all is sweetness and delicacy and harmony, and there are no red-headed clients to vex us with their conundrums."

My friend was an enthusiastic musician, being himself not only a very capable performer but a composer of no ordinary merit. All the afternoon he sat in the stalls wrapped in the most perfect happiness, gently waving his long, thin fingers in time to the music, while his gently smiling face and his languid, dreamy eyes were as unlike those of Holmes the sleuth-hound, Holmes the relentless, keen-witted, ready-handed criminal agent, as it was possible to conceive. In his singular character the dual nature alternately asserted itself, and his extreme exactness and astuteness represented, as I have often thought, the reaction against the poetic and contemplative mood which occasionally predominated in him. The swing of his nature took him from extreme languor to devouring energy; and, as I knew well, he was never so truly formidable as when, for days on end, he had been lounging in his armchair amid his improvisations and his black-letter editions. Then it was that the lust of the chase would suddenly come upon him, and that his brilliant reasoning power would rise to the level of intuition, until those who were unacquainted with his methods would look askance at him as on a man whose knowledge was not that of other mortals. When I saw him that afternoon so enwrapped in the music at St. James's Hall I felt that an evil time might be coming upon those whom he had set himself to hunt down.

"You want to go home, no doubt, Doctor," he remarked as we emerged.

"Yes, it would be as well."

"And I have some business to do which will take some hours. This business at Coburg Square is serious."

"Why serious?"

"A considerable crime is in contemplation. I have every reason to believe that we shall be in time to stop it. But to-day being Saturday rather complicates matters. I shall want your help to-night."

"At what time?"

"Ten will be early enough."

"I shall be at Baker Street at ten."

"Very well. And, I say, Doctor, there may be some little danger, so kindly put your army revolver in your pocket." He waved his hand, turned on his heel, and disappeared in an instant among the crowd.

I trust that I am not more dense than my neighbours, but I was always oppressed with a sense of my own stupidity in my dealings with Sherlock Holmes. Here I had heard what he had heard, I had seen what he had seen, and yet from his words it was evident that he saw clearly not only what had happened but what was about to happen, while to me the whole business was still confused and grotesque. As I drove home to my house in Kensington I thought over it all, from the extraordinary story of the red-headed copier of the *Encyclopedia* down to the visit to Saxe-Coburg Square, and the ominous words with which he had parted from me. What was this nocturnal expedition, and why should I go armed? Where were we going, and what were we to do? I had the hint from Holmes that this smooth-faced pawnbroker's assistant was a formidable man—a man who might play a deep game. I tried to puzzle it out, but gave it up in despair and set the matter aside until night should bring an explanation.

It was a quarter-past nine when I started from home and made my way across the Park, and so through Oxford Street to Baker Street. Two hansoms were standing at the door, and as I entered the passage I heard the sound of voices from above. On entering his room, I found Holmes in animated conversation with two men, one of whom I recognized as Peter Jones, the official police agent, while the other was a long, thin, sad-faced man, with a very shiny hat and oppressively respectable frock-coat.

"Ha! Our party is complete," said Holmes, buttoning up his pea-jacket and taking his heavy hunting crop from the rack. "Watson, I think you know Mr. Jones, of Scotland Yard? Let me introduce you to Mr. Merryweather, who is to be our companion in to-night's adventure."

"We're hunting in couples again, Doctor, you see," said Jones in his consequential way. "Our friend here is a wonderful man for starting a chase. All he wants is an old dog to help him to do the running down."

"I hope a wild goose may not prove to be the end of our chase," observed Mr. Merryweather gloomily.

"You may place considerable confidence in Mr. Holmes, sir," said the police agent loftily. "He has his own little methods, which are, if he won't mind my saying so, just a little too theoretical and fantastic, but he has the makings of a detective in him. It is not too much to say that once or twice, as in that business of the Sholto murder and the Agra treasure, he has been more nearly correct than the official force."

"Oh, if you say so, Mr. Jones, it is all right," said the stranger with deference. "Still, I confess that I miss my rubber. It is the first Saturday night for seven-and-twenty years that I have not had my rubber."

"I think you will find," said Sherlock Holmes, "that you will play for a higher stake to-night than you have ever done yet, and that the play will be more exciting. For you, Mr. Merryweather, the stake will be some £30,000; and for you, Jones, it will be the man upon whom you wish to lay your hands."

"John Clay, the murderer, thief, smasher, and forger. He's a young man, Mr. Merryweather, but he is at the head of his profession, and I would rather have my bracelets on him than on any criminal in London. He's a remarkable man, is young John Clay. His grandfather was a royal duke, and he himself has been to Eton and Oxford. His brain is as cunning as his fingers, and though we meet signs of him at every turn, we never know where to find the man himself. He'll crack a crib in Scotland one week, and be raising money to build an orphanage in Cornwall the next. I've been on his track for years and have never set eyes on him yet."

"I hope that I may have the pleasure of introducing you to-night. I've had one or two little turns also with Mr. John Clay, and I agree with you that he is at the head of his profession. It is past ten, however, and quite time that we started. If you two will take the first hansom, Watson and I will follow in the second."

Sherlock Holmes was not very communicative during the long drive and lay back in the cab humming the tunes which he had heard in the afternoon. We rattled through an endless labyrinth of gas-lit streets until we emerged into Farrington Street.

"We are close there now," my friend remarked. "This fellow Merryweather is a bank director, and personally interested in the matter. I thought it as well to have Jones with us also. He is not a bad fellow, though an absolute imbecile in his profession. He has one positive virtue. He is as brave as a bulldog and as tenacious as a lobster if he gets his claws upon anyone. Here we are, and they are waiting for us."

We had reached the same crowded thoroughfare in which we had found ourselves in the morning. Our cabs were dismissed, and, following the guidance of Mr. Merryweather, we passed down a narrow passage and through a side door, which he opened for us. Within there was a small corridor, which ended in a very massive iron gate. This also was opened, and led down a flight of winding stone steps, which terminated at another formidable gate. Mr. Merryweather stopped to light a lantern, and then conducted us down a dark, earth-smelling passage, and so, after opening a third door, into a huge vault or cellar, which was piled all round with crates and massive boxes.

"You are not very vulnerable from above," Holmes remarked as he held up the lantern and gazed about him.

"Nor from below," said Mr. Merryweather, striking his stick upon the flags which lined the floor. "Why, dear me, it sounds quite hollow!" he remarked, looking up in surprise.

"I must really ask you to be a little more quiet!" said Holmes severely. "You have already imperiled the whole success of our expedition. Might I beg that you would have the goodness to sit down upon one of those boxes, and not to interfere?"

The solemn Mr. Merryweather perched himself upon a crate, with a very injured expression upon his face, while Holmes fell upon his knees upon the floor and, with the lantern and a magnifying lens, began to examine minutely the cracks between the stones. A few seconds sufficed to satisfy him, for he sprang to his feet again and put his glass in his pocket.

"We have at least an hour before us," he remarked, "for they can hardly take any steps until the good pawnbroker is safely in bed. Then they will not lose a minute, for the sooner they do their work the longer time they will have for their escape. We are at present, Doctor— as no doubt you have divined—in the cellar of the City branch of one of the principal London banks. Mr. Merryweather is the chairman of directors, and he will explain to you that there are reasons why the more daring criminals of London should take a considerable interest in this cellar at present."

"It is our French gold," whispered the director. "We have had several warnings that an attempt might be made upon it."

"Your French gold?"

"Yes. We had occasion some months ago to strengthen our resources and borrowed for that purpose 30,000 napoleons from the Bank of France. It has become known that we have never had occasion to unpack the money, and that it is still lying in our cellar. The crate upon which I sit contains 2,000 napoleons packed between layers of lead foil. Our reserve of bullion is much larger at present than is usually kept in a single branch office, and the directors have had misgivings upon the subject."

"Which were very well justified," observed Holmes. "And now it is time that we arranged our little plans. I expect that within an hour matters will come to a head. In the meantime Mr. Merryweather, we must put the screen over that dark lantern."

"And sit in the dark?"

"I am afraid so. I had brought a pack of cards in my pocket, and I thought that, as we were a *partie carrée*, you might have your rubber after all. But I see that the enemy's preparations have gone so far that we cannot risk the presence of a light. And, first of all, we must choose our positions. These are daring men, and though we shall take them at a disadvantage, they may do us some harm unless we are careful. I shall stand behind this crate, and do you conceal yourselves behind those. Then, when I flash a light upon them, close in swiftly. If they fire, Watson, have no compunction about shooting them down."

I placed my revolver, cocked, upon the top of the wooden case behind which I crouched. Holmes shot the slide across the front of his lantern and left us in pitch darkness—such an absolute darkness as I have never before experienced. The smell of hot metal remained to assure us that the light was still there, ready to flash out at a moment's notice. To me, with my nerves worked up to a pitch of expectancy, there was something depressing and subduing in the sudden gloom, and in the cold dank air of the vault.

"They have but one retreat," whispered Holmes. "That is back through the house into Saxe-Coburg Square. I hope that you have done what I asked you, Jones?"

"I have an inspector and two officers waiting at the front door."

"Then we have stopped all the holes. And now we must be silent and wait."

What a time it seemed! From comparing notes afterwards it was but an hour and a quarter, yet it appeared to me that the night must have almost gone, and the dawn be breaking above us. My limbs were weary and stiff, for I feared to change my position; yet my nerves were worked up to the highest pitch of tension, and my hearing was so acute that I could not only hear the gentle breathing of my companions, but I could distinguish the deeper, heavier in-breath of the bulky Jones from the thin, sighing note of the bank director. From my position I could look over the case in the direction of the floor. Suddenly my eyes caught the glint of a light.

At first it was but a lurid spark upon the stone pavement. Then it lengthened out until it became a yellow line, and then, without any warning or sound, a gash seemed to open and a hand appeared, a white, almost womanly hand, which felt about in the center of the little area of light. For a minute or more the hand, with its writhing fingers, protruded out of the floor. Then it was withdrawn as suddenly as it appeared, and all was dark again save the single lurid spark which marked a chink between the stones.

Its disappearance, however, was but momentary. With a rending, tearing sound, one of the broad, white stones turned over upon its side and left a square, gaping hole, through which streamed the light of a lantern. Over the edge there peeped a clean-cut, boyish face, which looked keenly about it, and then, with a hand on either side of the aperture, drew itself shoulder-high and waist-high, until one knee rested upon the edge. In another instant he stood at the side of the hole and was hauling after him a companion, lithe and small like himself, with a pale face and a shock of very red hair.

"It's all clear," he whispered. "Have you the chisel and the bags? Great Scott! Jump, Archie, jump, and I'll swing for it!"

Sherlock Holmes had sprung out and seized the intruder by the collar. The other dived down the hole, and I heard the sound of rending cloth as Jones clutched at his skirts. The light flashed upon the barrel of a revolver, but Holmes' hunting crop came down on the man's wrist, and the pistol clinked upon the stone floor.

"It's no use, John Clay," said Holmes blandly. "You have no chance at all."

"So I see," the other answered with the utmost coolness. "I fancy that my pal is all right, though I see you have got his coat-tails."

"There are three men waiting for him at the door," said Holmes.

"Oh, indeed! You seem to have done the thing very completely. I must compliment you."

"And I you," Holmes answered. "Your red-headed idea was very new and effective."

"You'll see your pal again presently," said Jones. "He's quicker at climbing down holes than I am. Just hold out while I fix the derbies."

"I beg that you will not touch me with your filthy hands," remarked our prisoner as the handcuffs clattered upon his wrists. "You may not be aware that I have royal blood in my veins. Have the goodness, also, when you address me always to say 'sir' and 'please.'"

"All right," said Jones with a stare and a snigger. "Well, would you please, sir, march upstairs, where we can get a cab to carry your Highness to the police-station?"

"That is better," said John Clay serenely. He made a sweeping bow to the three of us and walked quietly off in the custody of the detective.

"Really, Mr. Holmes," said Mr. Merryweather as we followed them from the cellar, "I do not know how the bank can thank you or repay you. There is no doubt that you have detected and defeated in the most complete manner one of the most determined attempts at bank robbery that have ever come within my experience."

"I have had one or two little scores of my own to settle with Mr. John Clay," said Holmes. "I have been at some small expense over this matter, which I shall expect the bank to refund, but beyond that I am amply repaid by having had an experience which is in many ways unique, and by hearing the very remarkable narrative of the Red-headed League."

"You see, Watson," he explained in the early hours of the morning as we sat over a glass of whisky and soda in Baker Street, "it was perfectly obvious from the first that the only possible object of this rather fantastic business of the advertisement of the League, and the copying of the *Encyclopedia*, must be to get this not over-bright pawnbroker out of the way for a number of hours every day. It was a curious way of managing it, but, really, it would be difficult to suggest a better. The method was no doubt suggested to Clay's ingenious mind by the color of his accomplice's hair. The £4 a week was a lure which must draw him, and what was it to them, who were playing for thousands? They put in the advertisement, one rogue has the temporary office, the other rogue incites the man to apply for it, and together they manage to secure his absence every morning in the week. From the time that I heard of the assistant having come for half wages, it was obvious to me that he had some strong motive for securing the situation."

"But how could you guess what the motive was?"

"Had there been women in the house, I should have suspected a mere vulgar intrigue. That, however, was out of the question. The man's business was a small one, and there was nothing in his house which could account for such elaborate preparations, and such an expenditure as they were at. It must, then, be something out of the house. What could it be? I thought of the assistant's fondness for photography, and his trick of vanishing into the cellar. The cellar! There was the end of this tangled clue. Then I made inquiries as to this mysterious assistant and found that I had to deal with one of the coolest and most daring criminals in London. He was doing something in the cellar—something which took many hours a day for months on end. What could it be, once more? I could think of nothing save that he was running a tunnel to some other building.

"So far I had got when we went to visit the scene of action. I surprised you by beating upon the pavement with my stick. I was ascertaining whether the cellar stretched out in front or behind. It was not in front. Then I rang the bell, and, as I hoped, the assistant answered it. We have had some skirmishes, but we had never set eyes upon each other before. I hardly looked at his face. His knees were what I wished to see. You must yourself have remarked how worn, wrinkled, and stained they were. They spoke of those hours of burrowing. The only remaining point was what they were burrowing for. I walked round the corner, saw the City and Suburban Bank abutted on our friend's premises, and felt that I had solved my problem. When you drove home after the concert I called upon Scotland Yard and upon the chairman of the bank directors, with the result that you have seen."

"And how could you tell that they would make their attempt to-night?" I asked.

"Well, when they closed their League offices that was a sign that they cared no longer about Mr. Jabez Wilson's presence—in other words, that they had completed their tunnel. But it was essential that they should use it soon, as it might be discovered, or the bullion might be removed. Saturday would suit them better than any other day, as it would give them two days for their escape. For all these reasons I expected them to come to-night."

"You reasoned it out beautifully," I exclaimed in unfeigned admiration. "It is so long a chain, and yet every link rings true."

"It saved me from ennui," he answered, yawning. "Alas! I already feel it closing in upon me. My life is spent in one long effort to escape from the commonplaces of existence. These little problems help me to do so."

"And you are a benefactor of the race," said I.

He shrugged his shoulders. "Well, perhaps, after all, it is of some little use," he remarked. " '*L'homme c'est rien—l'oeuvre c'est tout*,' as Gustave Flaubert wrote to George Sand."

Printed in Great Britain
by Amazon

19823323R00078